**'You know nothing about me,'
Livvy told him huskily.**

'The pouting, wide-eyed, just-got-out-of-bed look does have a certain appeal to inexperienced boys. Fortunately one grows out of it with maturity.'

Livvy could hardly believe what she was hearing. The way she had just heard herself described bore so little resemblance to the truth that in any other circumstances she would have found it laughable . . .

Dear Reader

As Easter approaches, Mills & Boon are delighted to present you with an exciting selection of sixteen new titles. Why not take a trip to our Euromance locations—Switzerland or western Crete, where romance is celebrated in great style! Or maybe you'd care to dip into the story of a family feud or a rekindled love affair? Whatever tickles your fancy, you can always count on love being in the air with Mills & Boon!

The Editor

Born in Preston, Lancashire, **Penny Jordan** now lives with her husband in a beautiful fourteenth-century house in rural Cheshire. Penny has been writing for over ten years and now has over seventy novels to her name including the phenomenally successful POWER PLAY and SILVER. With over thirty million copies of her books in print and translations into seventeen languages, she has firmly established herself as a novelist of great scope.

FRENCH LEAVE

BY
PENNY JORDAN

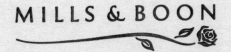

MILLS & BOON

MILLS & BOON LIMITED
ETON HOUSE, 18-24 PARADISE ROAD
RICHMOND, SURREY TW9 1SR

First published in Great Britain 1994
by Mills & Boon Limited

© Penny Jordan 1994

Australian copyright 1994
Philippine copyright 1994
This edition 1994

ISBN 0 263 78446 0

Set in Times Roman 10 on 12 pt.
01-9404-51794 C

Made and printed in Great Britain

CHAPTER ONE

LIVVY exhaled gratefully as she stopped her small car in the car park of the *auberge*. There were several other cars there with GB plates in addition to her own, she noticed as she got out and locked her door, but then the town was a popular stopping-off place for people *en route*, like herself, for the Dordogne.

She was glad now that she had had the foresight to book ahead for her one-night stay. She made a small moue as she picked up her overnight case, a tall slender woman in her mid-twenties with long, thick sunlight-streaked honey-blonde hair and intelligent wide-apart sherry-gold eyes.

No doubt there were those who would laugh at her far-sightedness, claiming that it was typical behaviour of her type: a teacher, a woman who liked uniformity and discipline in her life.

Those who thought like that didn't realise what modern teaching was like, she reflected ruefully as she headed for the *auberge*. These days it could be more like a mental obstacle course designed to test even the strongest of temperaments.

She was lucky she had established a rapport with her current batch of pupils. If she took the promotion she had been offered, to assistant head, she might lose that.

She was supposed to be on holiday, she reminded herself sternly, even if one of the reasons she had given way to her cousin Gale's insistence that she come to

France and housesit for her while she sorted out her marital problems was the fact that the solitude of a small remote farm in the heart of the Dordogne would allow her the space to think through what it was she actually wanted from her career. Advancement to assistant head and the potential consequent loss of hands-on teaching experience, or...

Or what? Staying where she was, continuing to teach French?

She paused appreciatively, sniffing the evening air; it had that indefinable tang which she felt she would have recognised anywhere, even blindfolded and gagged, as being quintessentially French.

Her smile changed to a frown as a huge BMW swept into the car park, coming perilously close to her. The driver's window was open, and through it she could see the harsh, almost hawklike profile of the man driving it. His hair was dark and thick, and something, an unfamiliar and disturbing *frisson* of sensation, tensed her spine as he turned and looked arrogantly at her. Perhaps because she was tired from her journey, or perhaps because something about him unsettled her, Livvy found herself immediately reacting to his lordly assumption that she would move out of his way.

Without pausing to think, instead of stepping back from the car she stepped up to it, gritting her teeth as she told him acidly, 'This happens to be a car park, not the Le Mans circuit, just in case you weren't aware of it.'

At close hand his appearance was even more harshly male than she had first realised, his eyes cold chips of hard ice in an angrily dangerous face, and a mouth with a bottom lip full enough to be shockingly sensual even when it was pulled in a hard line of keen dislike.

His eyes assessed her... assessed and dismissed her, Livvy recognised.

'How kind of you to put yourself out so much on my behalf.' The laid-back drawl wasn't quite soft enough to mask the hard edge to his voice, and Livvy only just managed to stop herself from flinching visibly as it hardened and crackled with acid contempt when he added, 'Perhaps it would have been safer and wiser to have used the footpath marked instead of the roadway. That way both of us would have been spared an unnecessary and unwanted altercation.'

He was driving on, closing his window, his face turned firmly away from her before she could make any response, leaving her gaping after him like an idiot, Livvy acknowledged, as she turned her head in the direction he had indicated and a wash of hot, embarrassed colour and the awareness that she had been the one in the wrong swept over her as she saw the footpath sign leading towards the *auberge* entrance.

What on earth had possessed her to challenge him like that in the first place? she asked herself irritably as she quickly hurried towards the footpath. It was so unlike her. Confrontation was normally not something she enjoyed and certainly never normally provoked, but there had been something about him... something about his attitude, his arrogance which had sparked off that fierce feeling of resentment inside her.

The disdain she had seen in his eyes as he drove past her had somehow become translated into something more personal, a disdain for her rather than for the world in general.

Now you are being ridiculous, she told herself firmly as she went into the *auberge* and up to the reception desk, giving her name in her fluent French, which came not just from studying the language but from having spoken it as a second language all her life. Her grand-mother had been French and consequently not just Livvy but all the grandchildren, including Gale, had learned to speak the language as a matter of course...

Gale too had used it as a career before she had married George, not as a teacher like Livvy but as an interpreter working in Brussels. Her cousin had been a very high-powered career woman before she made the unexpected announcement, at thirty, that she was to marry George.

Apart from her, virtually everyone else in the family was a little in awe of Gale, including her husband and children. She had that effect on people, Livvy admitted, and she thrived on it.

Livvy was made of sterner stuff, though; her job as a teacher had seen to that. On the surface she might seem to give way to her cousin's forceful demands simply to keep the peace, but Livvy's outwardly placid nature masked a very strong will, and she never allowed Gale to get away with manipulating her the way she did other people. Take this 'holiday', for instance...

Livvy smiled as the receptionist handed her her key and explained that if she wanted to have dinner she would have to order within the next hour.

Thanking her, Livvy went up to her room. She would unpack later, she told herself, mindful of the reception-ist's warning. It had been a long time since she had eaten lunch and she was very hungry. Quickly brushing her hair, she grinned to herself as she saw her reflection in the mirror. Leggings and a soft, casual, baggy sweater might be the accepted uniform of nearly every female under forty, but Livvy suspected that if the pupils of Form IV could see her right now her appearance would surprise them.

Fully aware of how very youthful she actually looked for her age, Livvy was always meticulous about wearing formal, authoritarian clothes for school. Soft sloppy sweaters knitted in a fabric that looked as though it wanted to be touched, cut-off leggings in a mass of brilliant colours which complemented the sweater, her hair loose instead of being neatly confined; no, this was not an image of her that her pupils would recognise.

It was amazing *how* different casual clothes made her feel, how much more relaxed. She enjoyed her job, but the tension of it, the need to exert discipline and to command her pupils' respect, could be very wearing at times, and it was a luxury to switch off that side of herself and to allow herself instead just simply to *be*.

A luxury indeed, and one that was having slightly disconcerting consequences, she reflected ten minutes later as she went back downstairs and found herself the subject of some unabashed and frankly appreciative male scrutiny from the two middle-aged men who had just walked into the hotel.

Their interest, flattering rather than threatening, increased her sense of well-being.

The *auberge*'s dining-room smelled appetisingly of French cooking. The early diners had finished and were just beginning to leave.

Livvy was shown to a small, comfortable table by one of the waiters. He spoke to her in such painstakingly careful English and with such pride that she hadn't the heart to reply to him in her own perfect French, instead waiting patiently while he stumbled over some of the words, resisting the impulse to help him. She was not here as a teacher, she told herself firmly as she gave him her order.

While she waited for her meal to be served, there was a small commotion in the doorway as four rowdy French youths pushed past the waiter, who was trying to stop them from entering.

To judge from the state of them, if they weren't actually drunk, then they certainly had been drinking, Livvy reflected. Their voices were loud, the language they were using vulgar and their opinion of the English tourists whose cars filled the car park and who sat nervously at their tables with their round-eyed children were stated in language which was not that which Livvy taught to her pupils.

To judge from the expressions of the other obviously British families dining, although they were aware of the youths' aggression, their command of the language wasn't sufficient for them to understand what was being said, which was probably just as well for Anglo-French relations, Livvy reflected as she firmly directed her attention to her own meal and away from the trouble that was obviously brewing.

The waiter had summoned the *auberge* owner, who now appeared to wrathfully chastise the young men, one of whom, Livvy recognised from their conversation, was apparently his son.

He was younger than the other three, eighteen or nineteen to their twenty-three or -four. In fact they were not as young as she had first supposed, Livvy realised, and because of that potentially rather more threatening.

The *auberge* owner was still trying to persuade them to leave, but now his son was insisting that they wanted to eat, demanding to know if his money and that of his friends was not just as good as that of the fat British tourists he seemed to favour so much.

The father gave way, casting anxious looks in the direction of the other guests, no doubt hoping that they could not, as she could, understand what was being said about them.

As they walked past her table, one of them, the oldest and most obnoxious, bumped into her table and then steadied himself against it.

Calmly Livvy went on with her meal. Common sense told her that the wisest and most sensible thing to do was not to make a fuss but simply to pretend he wasn't there.

She had forgotten, though, that he was not the same age as her pupils, and that she was not dressed in her normal authoritative way, and, as he straightened up and made a drunken apology, to her fury she also heard him make a comment about her breasts that was both over-familiar and exceedingly coarse.

It was only the discipline of three years of teaching that prevented her from reacting, not just by furiously objecting to what he had said, but from allowing the hot stinging surge of mortified feminine colour to burn up under her skin.

Like all women, she had experienced unwanted male comments about her body before, but this was different; for one thing what he had said was a good deal more crude than the normal joking and sometimes funny remarks called out by van drivers and building site workers, and for another...

For another, she was unpleasantly aware of the man's leering enjoyment of her defencelessness, his awareness not just of her inability to physically punish him for his rudeness, but of the fact that the manager appeared too afraid to challenge him either.

The temptation to stand up and demand the *auberge* owner call the *gendarmerie* was almost too strong for Livvy to resist, but then she reminded herself that she was on holiday and inevitably any kind of formal charge made now would result in delay to her resuming her journey in the morning.

Much as it irked her, she decided that on this occasion she would simply have to do nothing, other than finish her meal as quickly as she could and leave the dining-room.

Ten minutes later she realised that was not going to be so easy, and wished a little bitterly that she had demanded that something was done earlier, when the hotel owner had still been there for her to make demands on.

The little waiter who had been serving her was plainly terrified of the quartet; the other diners, like her, had obviously decided to finish their meals just as quickly as they could, and as the dining-room rapidly emptied Livvy felt disconcertingly conscious of the fact that she was soon going to be the only other occupant of the room.

The leader of the quartet was still making comments about her to his companions. She tried to comfort herself by reminding herself that he would only feel free to say things that were so vulgar and crass because he did not know she spoke French herself.

As a teacher, she was used to adolescent male aggression and thought she had learned to cope with it, but this was something different, she recognised. He was not an adolescent—here she had no authority...here, as his lewd, disgusting comments were making so plainly obvious, she was just another vulnerable, available woman.

She pushed her plate away, her appetite gone. Much as it went against the grain to be seen to be running away from them, she knew she had to go. The restaurant no longer felt safe; in fact it had become an alien, hostile place. All her feminine instincts warned her to leave. She got up as quietly and calmly as she could, ignoring the comments being shouted at her. Out of the corner of her eye she saw her tormentor stand up, but she refused either to turn her head or to be betrayed into showing any fear.

Her room key was in her handbag, but as she heard the restaurant door open behind her she still walked over to the reception desk and asked the clerk behind it,

'Are there any messages for me? It's room number twenty-four.'

She knew of course that there would not be any messages, but standing at the desk gave her a legitimate reason for turning round and checking that she wasn't being followed.

And if she was and he overheard her asking for messages, hopefully it might make him think that she was not, after all, alone.

'No, there is none,' the clerk told her, having checked the slot.

The leader of the quartet had left the restaurant after her and now he was standing several feet away, grinning insolently at her, but to her relief, although he paused with deliberate mockery as he drew level with her, he didn't make any further attempt to speak to her or touch her, simply moving on.

Thanking the clerk, Livvy hurried towards the stairs. Her bedroom had a good, firm lock on it and she intended to make sure she used it.

As luck would have it, her room was the last one along the corridor, right opposite the fire escape. Later she told herself that if she had been more alert she would have remembered that fact and acted accordingly, but as it was, when she finally reached her door, she simply gave a small pent-up sigh of relief, turned her back to the fire escape and opened her bag for her key, while keeping a strategic eye on the corridor to make sure that she hadn't been followed.

Because of this, it came as even more of a shock when she was grabbed from behind, her attacker laughing triumphantly as he swung her round to face him, pressing her body up against the wall with the weight of his while he taunted her with having tricked her...

He looked even less appealing close up than he had done in the restaurant, Livvy acknowledged as she fought down her panic and tried not to wince as he breathed garlic- and onion-laced fumes into her face.

His hands were round her forearms, exerting a pressure which would leave her with bruises, the weight of his body imprisoning her against the wall.

She didn't make the mistake of trying to fight him, sensing that that was just what he wanted, that he would relish the opportunity physically to subdue her. He was talking to her, laughing at her as he told her in explicit detail what he intended to do to her. Fear flickered inside her, spreading a numbing, dangerous paralysis through her body, and yet at the same time she felt oddly distanced from what was happening, apart from it, the enormity of it such that a part of her brain simply refused to accept it was happening.

As he ground his hips against her body she tensed in rejection. The door opposite her own opened and the hand that had been groping for her breast stilled.

Livvy was just about to call out thankfully for help to the man emerging from the room to place his breakfast menu on the door-handle when she recognised him.

It was the man from the car park, the one who had arrogantly let her see how insignificant he had thought her.

He was wearing a towelling robe open to the waist, revealing hard, tanned skin roughened by silky, dark hair.

A tiny *frisson* of unfamiliar sensation ran through her. The man holding her bent his head and tried to kiss her, muttering loudly, 'You know you want it. Downstairs you were showing it. Well, it won't be long now, *chérie*, and I promise you I'll show you what it's like to have a real man, a Frenchman.'

Across the few feet separating them, Livvy could see the disgust in the other man's eyes, the contempt. The man holding her was still talking, pouring out a stream of sexual obscenities which he appeared to deem suitable seduction talk.

The disgust on their observer's face deepened. He had the most extraordinarily powerful, harsh bone-structure, Livvy recognised, and such an air of cold austerity about him that the look he was giving her actually made her feel as though the temperature had physically dropped.

As he turned his back on them and returned to his room, closing the door behind him, her awareness that he had dared to assume that she wanted the Frenchman's

obnoxious caresses made Livvy so angry that she was
actually physically able to take him off guard and push
him off her.

She wasn't sure which of them was the more surprised
by her show of strength, she or he. He stared at her and
then shook his head, cursing her under his breath as he
came towards her.

Livvy was not going to be taken off guard a second
time. She bunched her fists as aggressively as she could,
facing him down, speaking to him in French as she told
him that she was going to report him to the police.

He was obviously shocked to hear her speaking perfect
French, but Livvy doubted if that would have been
enough to give her time to escape from him if the hotel
manager and one of the waiters hadn't suddenly emerged
from the fire escape to take hold of him and forcibly
march him away.

The manager returned later to apologise. He would
not blame her if she went ahead and pressed charges, he
told Livvy.

'By rights I ought to do so,' she returned crisply, 'if
only to ensure that some other woman doesn't suffer the
same fate, but since I can't afford to delay my journey
I shall have to leave it to *monsieur* to see that he is fit-
tingly punished. He seems a rather old companion for
your son,' she added pointedly.

A long discussion about the problems of bringing up
teenagers followed, leaving Livvy wishing she had simply
closed her door and wished *le patron* a goodnight. The
incident had shaken her more than she realised, she admitted as she prepared for bed. She was jumping at every
tiny, unfamiliar sound and had been twice to check that
the door was securely locked.

Additionally, for the first time in her life, she was going to sleep in a room with the windows closed. She might be on the second floor, but there was no point in taking any more risks, not after what had already happened. After all, as she had already discovered, she could scarcely rely on anyone to come to her rescue, could she?

She was still seething with bitter resentment over the reaction of the Englishman. How dared he assume that she had actually encouraged, never mind wanted, that lout's attack on her? Surely he could see that she had been struggling against him, not abandoning herself to the mindless passion he seemed to think she had been experiencing, if the disgust in his eyes had been anything to go by.

What kind of women was he used to, for heaven's sake, to have thought that?

The more she thought about the way he had behaved, the more angry Livvy became. She could have been raped and it would virtually have been his fault.

Much he would have cared what might have happened to her. Look at the way he had behaved in the car park—that should have warned her what kind of man he was. Arrogant pig. Thank goodness she had never been the type to be susceptible to that kind of darkly powerful male sexuality. It was personality that mattered to her, not looks. Uncomfortably, she suddenly remembered that odd and unwanted *frisson* of sensation she had experienced when he'd looked at her.

It had been caused by shock...fear...everyone knew that very strong emotions could have the most disconcerting effect on people. Her reaction had had nothing to do with the man himself. How could it have done? There had been nothing...nothing about him that she had found remotely attractive... nothing about him as a human being that could have caused that sharp, jagged lightning flash of sexual awareness.

She had probably imagined the whole thing... exaggerated the force of it. In her heightened emotional state it would have been strange if she had not done so, she comforted herself as she climbed back into bed.

She needed a good night's sleep if she was to be fresh for her journey in the morning. Resolutely she told herself to put the evening and its entire events firmly out of her mind.

An hour later she had to repeat this admonition more severely to herself; she reminded herself that she was a teacher, and a firm fan of self-discipline, someone who prided herself on her logical, calm approach to life's problems.

So what was going wrong? Why were the arrogant, contemptuous features of a certain man coming between her and her attempts to go to sleep? If the thought of anyone was keeping her awake, it should have been the man who had tried to attack her, but disconcertingly she could barely remember his features, while the other...the Englishman's were so firmly etched on her memory that she might have known him for years, not merely glimpsed him for a handful of seconds.

No doubt, after closing his door on her, he had not even given her a second thought.

Across the hallway in his own room, the object of her thoughts was also trying to sleep. He moved irritably in his bed, his body tense and unrelaxed. This was the last thing he needed.

The whole purpose of this trip to France was to allow him to unwind, to give him a small breathing space, not to...

Not to what? Make him remember things he'd far rather forget?

Damn that woman. He had known she was trouble the moment he saw her in the car park, standing there, all lissom, delicate, provocative feminine sensuality.

He had watched her walking away from him, her movements confirming what his senses had already told him.

She had look so vibrantly, so sensually alive, her hair an unfettered banner against the sky, her skin soft, glowing, her body...

He turned over, cursing. What the hell was wrong with him? He had seen for himself what type she was. That soft, full-lipped mouth was not as vulnerable as it looked, and certainly nowhere near as untutored.

He felt his muscles bunch. Why the hell hadn't she and the man she had so obviously picked up in the *auberge* waited to begin their lovemaking until they were inside her room? Lovemaking. What was it about some women that made them want to degrade themselves with that kind of involvement...?

To judge from the things her companion had been saying to her, theirs was no tender, emotional coming-together... He doubted that they had even bothered to exchange names.

He frowned as he turned his head towards the window. Why waste his time thinking about her...letting her get under his skin?

Why?

He already knew the answer, and it wasn't just that, for a moment, outside in the car park, not only his body but his senses as well had responded to the feminine sensuality of her.

It was well over a decade, thirteen years ago today to be exact, since the ending of his marriage. His marriage...what a farcical black comedy of errors that had been. What a fool he had been, to fall for one of the oldest tricks in the book.

She had been taking precautions, Claire had assured him tearfully, but something had gone wrong, and now she was pregnant with his child.

His child... He had had no option but to marry her.

Thirteen years, and surely in that time he had come far enough down life's road to know far better than to let himself be disturbed by his awareness of a woman, especially a woman like that one.

What would she have done if he had been the one to approach her, to...?

He cursed again. What in God's name was he thinking? He didn't want her really, of course he couldn't want a woman like that.

Could he?

CHAPTER TWO

ONE o'clock... Livvy sighed as she heard the town clock striking the hours, acknowledging that she was no closer to sleep now than she had been when she first came to bed.

And since she couldn't sleep, why waste time trying...? Why didn't she give some thought to the events which had brought her here to France instead?

Everything had happened in such a rush that she had barely had time to think everything through properly, a fact which her cousin Gale had used to her advantage, she reflected wryly as she admitted the way Gale had manoeuvred her into doing what she wanted.

Her pupils and her fellow teachers would have found it hard to believe that she had let Gale get her way so easily, but then the offer of several weeks' holiday in such a lovely part of France had been too tempting to resist, even if she had initially had doubts about the reasons Gale had given her for wanting her to stay at the farmhouse.

It had all started three weeks ago, when Gale had rung her and said that she needed to talk to her urgently.

This on its own had surprised her. Gale was not in the habit of needing to talk to anyone, much less her ten years younger and in her eyes far less worldly cousin.

At that stage, Livvy had assumed that the 'urgent talk' must have something to do with her nephews, and that Gale, who despite her husband George's having a well-paid job considered thrift not just a virtue but a positive pleasure, wanted to persuade her to give the boys some free private coaching.

Livvy had all her arguments ready. She was quite genuinely far too busy to be able to be of any help to her nephews. The fact that the long summer holidays were only three weeks away did not mean that she had time on her hands—far from it. Not only did she have to sit down and give some serious thought to whether or not she really wanted to take the job of assistant head which she had been offered, she also had to prepare the coming year's work.

However, once Gale, in her normal self-confident, slightly bossy way had told Livvy that her Busy Lizzie needed re-potting and that she had known she had been right to warn her not to paint her kitchen that bright yellow, Livvy discovered that it wasn't her sons whom Gale wanted to discuss, but her husband.

'I'm worried about George,' she announced once they were both settled in Livvy's pretty sitting-room with their cups of coffee.

Gale had disapproved of Livvy's choice of colour scheme for her small home. The soft pastel colours were not really suitable for a schoolteacher, Gale had told her; they did not create the right impression.

Livvy had laughed. Other members of the family often complained that Gale drove them mad with her bossiness, but Livvy liked her elder cousin and was often amused by her. Unlike other people, she refused to allow Gale to dominate her, dealing calmly and quietly with her cousin's dominating personality.

'There are other aspects to my life than my work,' she had pointed out mildly, when Gale had said that a stronger, more purposeful colour scheme would have been more appropriate.

What she hadn't gone on to say was that sometimes she needed the soft, pretty pastel comfort of her home, that sometimes, after a particularly difficult day at school, she needed to come home to a place that helped her to get back in touch with the more feminine and vulnerable side of her nature.

When she had first chosen teaching as her career, her counsellors had suggested that she might find the work too much of an emotional strain, that the work might be too stressful for someone of her rather gentle personality.

Being gentle was not the same thing as being weak, Livvy had countered. And in the years since she had qualified she had gone on to prove that her sometimes deceptively mild manner did not mean that she was incapable of exerting control and discipline.

Unlike Gale, Livvy had never felt any need to prove to others how strong-willed and dominant she was; it was enough that *she* know that, if necessary, she could summon up that strength from within herself.

Knowing that gave her a serenity that others often envied.

Not Gale, however. Gale, who for all her high IQ seemed to be pathetically lacking when it came to reading people's personalities.

Perhaps that was why *she* was inclined to make allowances for her, Livvy reflected. Where others saw Gale as a bossy, demanding woman who steamrollered over everyone around her, Livvy saw her as someone who had never known what it was to have the gift of being sensitive to others' feelings and, because of that, was disadvantaged.

'George!' she exclaimed in some surprise. 'What's wrong with him? Is he ill? Is he...?'

'Ill? No, he's not ill. But he's changed completely, Livvy. He's just not the man I married any more. Since the company was taken over last year...' She pursed her lips. 'Well, for a start we hardly ever get to see him any more, and when he is at home he locks himself away in his study, claiming that he needs to work. And now— would you believe?—he says that he wants to sell the farmhouse.'

'But you only bought it last year,' Livvy protested, remembering how thrilled and proud her cousin had been at its acquisition, and yes, perhaps a little boastful as well, but then that was Gale's way; material things were important to her.

'I know, but George claims that the loan he took out on it is costing him too much and that, with the boys about to go on to secondary school, the cost of their fees will mean that we have to cut down. I know for a fact that he's just had a very good rise, and if Peter passes his common entrance when he sits it he'll get a free place to Hadyards.'

'Times are hard and getting harder,' Livvy interrupted her firmly. 'George has always been financially cautious, and you did say yourself that the farmhouse needed completely renovating...'

'Yes, I know that, but there's more to it than that. George knows how much the farmhouse means to me, and to threaten to sell it when he knows that I don't want him to, and that I can't do a thing to stop him... He borrowed the money from the company, you see, and because of the legal ramifications the deeds are solely in his name. I'm not going to let him do it, though, Livvy, and I've warned him that if he tries... Look, what I want you to do is to go and stay there for a few weeks just to...'

'To what, Gale? I sympathise with you, but I can hardly stop George selling the place if that's what he intends to do.'

'No, but if you're there it will give me a breathing space... time to talk to him and make him see how unreasonable he's being. He's always had a soft spot for you, Livvy. I'll tell him that you need to get away somewhere peaceful because of all the stress of your job...'

'Gale,' Livvy protested warningly, 'I'm perfectly capable of dealing with any stress I might suffer from by myself, thank you very much.'

She could see from Gale's expression that her cousin knew she had pushed her too far. She changed tack.

'Please, Livvy. I wouldn't ask if it weren't so important to me. You know how I've always felt about France, and I know that you feel the same. It's a part of us, after all... of our heritage, and I want to pass that heritage on to the boys... I want *them* to experience at least a part of their childhood growing up in the French countryside as we did...'

Wryly, Livvy mentally acknowledged the skill of her cousin's argument. She *had* enjoyed those childhood times in France, and treasured the memory of them. They had given her a view of another nation's way of life that she felt had broadened her horizons and her awareness in a way that very few people were fortunate enough to experience.

'And it's not just that,' Gale continued, sensing victory. 'I'm not just being sentimental. There's the fact that their French is bound to improve, and by the time they're adults the ability to speak a second language will be a very important career asset. You're the one who's always said that the inability to understand one another's languages is one of the greatest barriers between peoples.'

'Yes, I know,' Livvy acknowledged.

'All I want is enough time to make George see reason... To make him listen... If only we could get away ourselves, but it's impossible at the moment. He's working virtually twenty-four hours a day. Ever since Robert Forrest took over the company...'

'Robert Forrest?' Livvy was interested.

'Yes. I told you, the millionaire entrepreneur who bought out the company last year. George thinks he's wonderful. Personally I blame *him* for the way George has changed, the way he's behaving. He's completely dominating George, making him work virtually twenty-four hours a day. Just because *he's* not married...

'At least, not any more. He was once, but his wife left him for someone else. Small wonder. She got an enormous divorce settlement, apparently. She's dead now... a car accident with her new man...'

She broke off as Livvy made a small sound of compassion and exclaimed, 'Poor man, what a dreadful thing to have happened. It's bound to have made him a bit bitter.'

'A bit *bitter*? The man's a misogynist. A marriage-wrecker,' Gale stormed. 'I'd love to tell him exactly what I think of him and what he's doing to our marriage... to our children. He hasn't got any of his own. Men like that never do, do they? Of course George defends him like a dog protecting a bone.' Her eyes flashed, her face flushing.

She was a very striking-looking woman...commanding rather than pretty. Despite Gale's bossy way, Livvy was genuinely fond of her cousin, who had been very generous with both her advice and more practical help in the form of rent-free accommodation in the early days when Livvy had first been teaching.

She was fond of George, too, and of their children, and a summer spent in the Dordogne *was* a tempting prospect.

There was nothing after all to keep her at home for the summer; no plans...no special relationship. Yes, a couple of months in the Dordogne was certainly a far more enticing prospect than the same period of time spent in her small flat.

Even so...

'Look, Gale, are you *sure* that you're not being a little bit unfair to George? With so many people losing their jobs...'

'Unfair?' Gale turned on her indignantly. 'Just how fair am I supposed to be? How fair is he being to us, to me? I told him, Livvy...I told him that he owed it to us to spend more time with us...that he was neglecting us and that if he wasn't careful he could lose us. I told him he had to tell Robert Forrest that he had a right to his private life; I even gave him an ultimatum and warned him that, unless he did so...' She broke off, shaking her head.

'That was last week, and since then nothing's changed...nothing. He left for work at seven o'clock

this morning and he won't be back until close on mid-
night. That's if I'm lucky...

'You tell me, Livvy. Am I being unfair?'

Sadly, Livvy shook her head. No, Gale wasn't being
unfair, she reflected later as she drove home. But she
could perhaps be more understanding...more compassionate...more aware? Wryly Livvy admitted that
the chances of her strong-minded cousin's exhibiting any
of those emotions were very slim indeed.

'Two months in the Dordogne, rent-free—you lucky
thing,' her colleagues had sighed enviously.

'Mmm...maybe you'll meet some gorgeous, sexy
Frenchman,' Jenny, the maths teacher, had teased her.

Livvy had laughed. 'We're talking about rural France,
not Paris,' she had told her. 'Any Frenchmen I do meet,
handsome or otherwise, will be very, very firmly attached to their wives and children.'

'So?' Jenny's eyes had twinkled. 'Who's talking about
anything permanent? What's wrong with a small summer
fling, an excitingly brief affair?'

'What's wrong with it is that I don't want it,' Livvy
told her firmly. 'Getting involved with a man who just
wants to use me isn't my idea of fun.'

'You might not be able to stop yourself. What if you
fall in love?'

'In *lust*, you mean,' Livvy had corrected her, shaking
her head as she added determinedly, 'No, I'd never do
that. My self-respect wouldn't let me. When I *do* love
a man it will be because I admire and respect him in-
tellectually and emotionally, not because I'm turned on
physically by his body...'

She had left the staff-room with Jenny's laughter still ringing in her ears.

'Be careful,' Jenny had called warningly after her. 'You could be tempting fate, saying something like that.'

'No way,' Livvy had responded with a grin. 'Tempting fate, or a Frenchman, is the last thing I intend to do!'

At twenty-five she considered herself far too responsible and mature to plunge into the kind of reckless, hedonistic, *dangerous* type of affair Jenny had teased her about. Such affairs, from what she had observed of them, inevitably led to someone being hurt, and badly, and she considered that she was far too cautious and self-protective by nature to risk bringing that kind of pain upon herself.

No, she would be far too busy preparing for the new term and thinking about her own future to have time for romance, even if it were something she wanted— which it wasn't.

Not that her time in France was going to be completely taken up with work, though: she had promised herself some relaxation, some sightseeing trips and explorations. She had even generously offered to take off Gale's shoulders the burden of liaising with the local tradesmen and suppliers in connection with some of the more urgent renovations Gale was organising, agreeing that it would be far easier for her to deal with the French contractors, since she was *in situ*.

'Are you sure you actually want to go ahead with these alterations?' she had asked her cousin when they had discussed Gale's plans for modernising the existing bathroom and adding a new one. 'After all, if George does insist on selling . . .'

'He won't. Not once I get him out of Robert Forrest's clutches for long enough to make him see sense. I shouldn't be surprised if *he's* the one who's turned George against the farmhouse in the first place; he's that kind of man,' she added darkly.

Livvy had given her a thoughtful look. She hoped Gale was right about being able to persuade George to keep the property, because she could tell how important it was to her. She understood Gale's desire for her sons to experience the same pleasure they had known as children, but at the same time she felt, fair-mindedly, that a smaller and more modest environment would provide those benefits just as well and be far less of a financial burden on George.

She wondered if Gale was right to lay the blame for George's changed behaviour at the feet of his new employer. As the victim of an unhappy marriage, it was perhaps only to be expected that he should have a bias against marriage and feel suspicious or antagonistic towards the female sex.

She hoped Gale would not ride too roughshod over George's views. He was a nice man and a good husband and father.

She stifled a yawn and moved sleepily beneath the duvet. The more she observed of other people's relationships, the more wary it made her of that kind of commitment. She was glad she was not the type to fall drastically and dangerously head over heels in love.

Beneath the bedclothes she gave a small shiver. Knowing *her* luck, if she did it would probably be with entirely the wrong type of man.

Like the one across the hallway, for instance? Ridiculous—what woman in her right senses would fall in love with a man like that, who for all his spectacular aura of raw masculinity and power had shown by his attitude that he had as much awareness of and respect for the female psyche as she had of what went on inside the head of a man-eating tiger?

No, if she ever did fall in love, it would be with someone compassionate and caring, intelligent and aware, a man who valued her as an equal human being, not one who dismissed her as a sexual object, condemning her with cold-eyed disgust.

The BMW was still in the car park when Livvy left early the next morning. She gave it a dismissive look as she walked virtuously past it, reflecting on the laziness of its slothful owner and the fact that he was missing what was for her one of the best parts of the day.

Well, at least she was unlikely to come into contact with him again, she reflected thankfully as she let herself into her own car and pulled on her seatbelt.

Having planned her route carefully in advance, Livvy didn't have any trouble in reaching Beaulieu, which was the nearest sizeable town to the farmhouse.

She ate a late lunch in the town and shopped for provisions, just enough to tide her over for the first couple of days. After all, one of the pleasures of being in France was the food. Her French grandmother had taught her how a Frenchwoman shopped and the important role that not just the consumption of food but its purchase and preparation played in the traditional French lifestyle.

It was mid-afternoon before she started the final part of her journey, taking her time as she carefully checked each road sign, not wanting to miss her way on the mass of narrow country roads which criss-crossed the countryside, and her diligence was finally rewarded when she drove into the small village closest to the farmhouse.

Although she had not visited it before, she had seen photographs of it and had agreed with Gale that it was idyllically situated, surrounded by lush countryside with a view looking out across a small tributary of the Dordogne river, its privacy assured by the farmland which surrounded it...

George had tentatively expressed the view that it might be a bit *too* isolated, but Gale had told him firmly that he was wrong and that its isolation only added to its appeal.

'For us, maybe,' George had conceded. 'But the children...'

'The children will love it,' Gale had interrupted him. 'Clean, fresh air, a simple country lifestyle will be very good for them; it's exactly what they need.'

Now, Livvy wondered if after all George might not have had a point. Isolation was all very well for adults, craving the peace and quiet of the countryside, but children... *teenagers*...

If he had, it wouldn't be easy getting Gale to acknowledge it, Livvy acknowledged. Rather sadly, Livvy wondered how much of the time George was giving to his work was actually being forced upon him by his new boss, and how much might be voluntary: a means of escape from a wife whose strong-mindedness might sometimes be rather wearying?

Just as she was beginning to wonder uneasily if she had after all taken a wrong turning, the thickly forested countryside through which she was travelling gave way to open land, the fields which Gale had told her went with the farmhouse and which, although presently neglected and unworked, she hoped to rent out to a local farmer.

'The money we get from letting the land will help to pay for the work on the farmhouse,' she had explained to Livvy.

Now in front of her she could see the shape of a building, its age betrayed by the soft, fading colour of the sandstone walls.

Thankfully, Livvy stopped her car in the unevenly flagged yard. It was just starting to grow dark, but there was still enough light for her to make her way to the heavy front door, the keys Gale had given her held firmly in her hand. Weeds had sprung up and rooted themselves firmly between the worn slabs of stone, evidence of the length of time the farm had been uninhabited.

Livvy was no stranger to rural France, although this was the first time she had visited the Dordogne, and she found the silence that surrounded her soothing rather than unnerving. She unlocked and opened the door, wincing as the unoiled hinges squeaked rustily.

The door opened directly into the kitchen, a large, rectangular-shaped room with small windows and a musty, slightly damp smell. As she switched on the light, Livvy winced a little in its harsh brightness.

'The kitchen will have to be completely refitted,' Gale had told her. 'I want something very simple and sturdy— a free-standing kitchen range would be ideal.'

'But very expensive,' Livvy had warned her.

'Mmm. Well, hopefully we'll be able to find someone local whom I can organise to make exactly what I want. The farmer we bought the house from has the most wonderful armoire, and there was a dresser in the kitchen. It shouldn't be too difficult to pick up some good antique pieces quite reasonably.'

Given her cousin's determination and energy, it probably wouldn't be too long before she did transform the kitchen, Livvy acknowledged, but right now...

It would probably look better in the morning when she had had a good night's sleep, Livvy acknowledged as she surveyed the grimy, deep porcelain sink and the old-fashioned cooking range.

The fridge-freezer standing in one corner of the room, attached to a large Calor gas canister, looked oddly incongruous, as did the small stove adjacent to it. Incongruous but very welcome, Livvy acknowledged as she saw the kettle standing on it and went to pick it up.

The water which spurted from the tap was icily cold and slightly brownish in colour. The farmhouse had neither mains water nor electricity, the former being supplied via its own well and the latter from a generator installed in one of the outbuildings.

While she was waiting for the kettle to boil, she might as well bring in her things, Livvy decided.

She had brought one small case with her; the rest of the space in her car had been filled with the boxes of bedding, towels, kitchen utensils, food and other items which Gale had insisted she bring with her.

Gale and George had bought the farmhouse complete with its furniture. Rubbish in the main, Gale had snorted, but the beds, heavy, old-fashioned affairs with wooden head- and foot-boards, had been worth keeping, although she had of course had to replace the mattresses.

The sturdy, worn stairs led up from a room adjacent to the kitchen, the British equivalent of a comfortable family breakfast-room.

Wearily, Livvy climbed them.

'You can use any bedroom you like,' Gale had told her. 'Although the double ones at the front have the best views.'

Livvy opened the first door she came to and switched on the light.

She would sleep well tonight, she acknowledged half an hour later when she had drunk her tea and finished making up the bed. She was almost too tired for even the briefest of sluices under the feeble trickle of the anti-quated shower, only habit compelling her to go through the motions of getting ready for bed.

Ten minutes later, her body still glowing from the rough towelling she had given it, she curled up gratefully under her duvet.

Tomorrow her holiday could begin properly. Her mouth watered as she contemplated the pleasure of eating croissants fresh from the *boulangerie*, washed down with rich, fragrant coffee.

Mmm...it would make a delicious and welcome change from her normal rushed breakfast of a few mouthfuls of muesli eaten hurriedly between checking her diary, reading her post and generally getting ready for work.

Livvy could hear a noise. A car door slamming. She sat up groggily in bed frowning as she glanced at her watch. It was just gone nine. She had slept for longer than she had intended.

As she climbed out of bed and reach for her cotton wrap, she wondered who her unexpected visitor was.

She guessed that it would probably be the farmer from whom Gale and George had bought the house. Gale had described him to her, fifty-odd, short and gnarled, very good at playing dumb when he chose and even, ridiculously, trying to pretend at times that he could not understand Gale's excellently fluent French, and with the financial acumen that many a finance director would envy.

Livvy smiled to herself now, remembering how she had guessed from the acid note of chagrin in Gale's voice that for once her cousin had met her match.

It was a pity she had overslept; if the Dordogne was anything like the other parts of rural France she had previously visited its inhabitants would operate a code of behaviour almost Victorian in its formality. Appearing to greet a neighbour a nine o'clock in the morning not dressed, her hair tousled and still half asleep, would doubtless reinforce the French belief in their superiority as a race.

She was halfway across the kitchen when she heard someone turning a key in the door lock.

Frowning, she stood still. It made sense that the farmer should have a key so that he could keep a check on the property while it was empty, but Gale had told her that she was going to warn him to expect her, and, even though she had parked her car out of sight in one of the outbuildings, surely he might at least have knocked first.

The door opened and Livvy froze in shocked disbelief.

It couldn't be, but it was: the man who had just let himself into the farmhouse was the same man she had seen at the *auberge* last night, the same man who had been so rude to her in the car park, the same man who had so contemptuously ignored her plight later.

As she stared into his cold, arrogantly handsome face and felt the shock of the invisible force-field which seemed to surround him, she was temporarily completely lost for words.

Distantly her mind registered the fact that, for some odd reason, her body was reacting to his presence in the most alarming and dangerous way.

Beneath her terry robe and the thin cotton T-shirt she had slept in, her nipples were peaking with unfamiliar and confusing intensity, a shock-wave of sensation exploding inside her.

Quickly, she pulled her robe protectively closer to her body. Her heart was beating fast and heavily; she felt confused and powerless, plunged into a situation which both alarmed and excited her.

What was he doing here? *How* had he found her? *Why* had he followed her?

Giddily her thoughts swirled dizzily through her brain, temporarily robbing her of her normal, calm control, and then chillingly she realised how dangerous the situation was, how vulnerable she was.

She was alone here, vulnerable and unprotected, and for all his apparent wealth and respectability he could ... he might ...

Firmly she swallowed back the fear and confronted him.

'Never allow yourself to be intimidated or to show fear. Never let anyone else take control from you,' she and her fellow students had been told before they went into teaching, and that advice applied just as much to this situation as it did to facing a class of pupils.

Forcing her tense throat muscles to relax, she demanded huskily, 'What are you doing here ... why have you followed me? If you don't leave immediately, I shall call the police.'

CHAPTER THREE

'FOLLOWED *you*?'

The harsh derision in his voice was as abrasive as sandpaper against vulnerable flesh, making Livvy wince and tense.

'You've got some nerve. If anyone will be calling the police it will be me. People like you who break into private property and squat... You've no right...'

Break in! *Squat*! Livvy was almost too angry to speak. How dared he accuse her?

'You're the one who has no right to be here,' she interrupted him furiously. 'Not me. This house belongs to my cousin and her husband and it was Gale who invited me to spend the summer here, and...'

'You're Gale's cousin?'

Against her will, Livvy found herself responding to the sharp authority of his tone, inclining her head in curt agreement as he cut across her angry speech. A persistent and unignorable warning bell was beginning to ring in her brain. 'You know Gale and George?' she demanded warily, trusting its authenticity.

'Yes,' came the terse response. 'What do you mean, Gale invited you to spend the summer here? George told me the house would be empty.'

Livvy swallowed.

'You will tell George that I'm going to be there, won't you?' she had asked her cousin.

'Of course I will,' Gale had reassured her. 'Once he can bring himself to spare us some of his precious time.'

As she looked into the face of the man watching her, the stark, cold realisation of why he was here suddenly struck her.

'George wanted to sell the farmhouse,' Gale had told her. Then Livvy had taken Gale's complaints about her husband with a pinch of salt, genuinely believing that George would never behave in such an underhand manner, but this man's presence here confirmed everything Gale had told her.

He *looked* the type who would take advantage of someone else's problems for his own pecuniary gain, she decided cynically.

Tilting her chin, she told him sweetly, 'Well, now you can see that it isn't, can't you? If you want to look round I can't stop you, but obviously I'd like you to leave as soon as possible...'

'Me, leave...? My arrangement with George was that I would stay here for a while...'

'Surely it doesn't take long for you to decide whether or not you want to buy the place?' she asked derisively. He certainly didn't look the indecisive type, far from it.

'To buy it?' He was frowning at her now, but Livvy wasn't deceived.

'Yes, and no doubt you're hoping to get it at less than the market value,' she added scathingly, her lip curling. 'I've met men like you before, men who are always looking to take advantage of other's misfortunes, men who put money and materialism above everything else. You should get on well with George's boss. He's another man who thinks that money and power are everything, who doesn't care about the effects his demands on the people who work for him could be having on their family lives.

'Yes ... You and Robert Forrest both obviously share the same lack of any real moral values.'

Livvy saw with some satisfaction that she had succeeded in silencing him. But not for long.

'Moral values? My God, that's rich, coming from someone like you,' he told her bitterly.

'What do you mean?' The moment she made the heated demand, Livvy knew she had done the wrong thing. She watched as the hostility in his eyes was overlaid with cynical contempt.

'Oh, come on. I saw you last night, remember? With your... friend. Tell me something, did you ever bother to wait long enough to find out his name before falling into bed with him? Good, was he? But hardly the type you'd want to take home with you? No, I expect that, like your cousin, when you find a fool besotted enough to marry you you'll make sure he's rich enough to support you.'

Livvy couldn't believe what she was hearing. How dared he make such allegations against her, misjudge her so unfairly, condemn her on such implausible evidence? His insults to her were too pathetic to warrant rejection, she decided shakily, but his remark about Gale...

'Gale did *not* marry George for his money,' she told him coldly.

'No? From what I've seen of your cousin, she's very good at spending her husband's money. Nor is she above blackmailing him if necessary by using their children.'

'Gale just wants the best for her sons. Any mother would,' Livvy protested, defending her cousin.

'The best for her sons and the best for herself, but where does George fit in? I doubt very much that she ever gives any thought to what he might want . . . to what might be best for him. It's no wonder . . .'

He stopped abruptly, frowning, absorbed in his own thoughts, Livvy recognised as she wondered uneasily exactly what they were. He seemed to know an awful lot about George and Gale. He also seemed to have a definite bias against her sex, Livvy reflected, and then wondered if it was women in general he felt contempt for, or merely Gale and herself in particular.

If so . . .

If so, what did it matter? She didn't know him, after all, and after the way he had just behaved and spoken she was heartily glad she wasn't likely to get to know him either.

She ought to feel sorry for him really, not angry with him. He really was the most abysmal judge of character, his judgement so flawed that in other circumstances his condemnation of her would almost have been laughable.

'I think you should leave,' she told him firmly. 'George ought to have checked with Gale before allowing you to come down here to inspect the property. Gale doesn't . . .'

'Gale doesn't what?' he challenged. 'Gale doesn't want him to sell it? Is that why she sent *you* here? To use your charm to persuade would-be buyers to change their minds.'

His mouth twisted in a way that made Livvy want to hit him as he said the word 'charm'. That he should have such a low opinion of her sex was his problem and not hers, she reminded herself, and there was at least one point she could correct him on.

'Gale did not *send* me here—for any purpose. I came of my own free will, because I wanted a quiet, peaceful, uninterrupted holiday on my own.'

He was not impressed. The look he gave her sent shivers icing down her back. It was so unkind, so feral almost.

He didn't like her defiant attitude, she could see it in his eyes, and with it an awareness of his sexual power and her potential weakness. It was totally unlike her to be so keenly aware of a man's sexuality, and totally inappropriate in these circumstances. It irked her, baffled her, angered her, and yet made her feel anxious as well that she should have this sharp, unwanted insight into the maleness he exuded.

Her heart was beating much faster than usual, and not just because she was so angry with him, she acknowledged. She had heard that anger could be a powerful aphrodisiac, but surely not when that anger was directed at a total stranger, and a man, moreover, who on the face of it had nothing about him other than the extraordinary strength of his sexuality to attract her?

And since when, anyway, had she been attracted by a man's sexuality? All her previous relationships had been based on mutual interests, mutual liking, mutual respect.

'A peaceful, solitary holiday...a woman like you?' he scoffed tauntingly now. 'Don't forget I saw you at the *auberge*.'

'You don't understand,' Livvy protested, and then stopped. Why should she bother to explain herself to him? If he hadn't been able to see with his own eyes what was actually happening, what chance was there of his listening while she tried to explain, and why should she anyway?

'No, I don't,' he agreed curtly and then, almost as though it was against his will, he added harshly, 'For God's sake, has it never occurred to you what risks you're running? Or is that all part of the excitement...the danger of not knowing...of living dangerously, taking risks?'

Too shocked to defend herself, Livvy stared at him. His teeth were white and strong. She gave a small, uncontrollable shudder, imagining their sharp bite against her skin...imagining...

'Gale can't stop George from selling this place, you know,' he warned her. 'He's under a great deal of stress at the moment, and——'

'Yes, because Robert Forrest is virtually making him work twenty-four hours a day,' Livvy interrupted him bitterly. 'All Gale wants is a chance to talk things over with him, but she barely sees him, he's so busy, never mind gets time to discuss anything with him.'

'The impression I have of your cousin isn't that of a woman who goes in much for discussion or compromise. If George is avoiding her, perhaps it's because he feels he has a good reason to do so.'

Livvy tensed. This man, whoever he was, seemed to know a good deal about her cousin's marriage, his words revealing vulnerabilities in it that Livvy hadn't known existed. Her stomach tensed uneasily; George and Gale had always seemed to have such a secure, sturdy marriage. Both of them were devoted to their sons. Livvy had seen far too often in her work as a teacher the effects of a parental break-up on children to want to see the same thing happen to her nephews.

'Gale loves George.' She could hear the anxiety and distress in her own voice.

'Does she? Or does she simply love the lifestyle he provides?'

'No,' Livvy denied vehemently. 'Gale had a good job of her own when she met George; she was financially independent. She gave that up to marry him, to be with him and the boys.'

'So if material things don't matter to her, why all the fuss about his wanting to sell this place?'

'Perhaps it's the fact that he's trying to sell it without consulting her,' Livvy told him, rallying. 'Going behind her back...deceiving her...not telling her that he had arranged for you——'

'Just as *she* didn't tell George that she had arranged for you to come here,' he interrupted her, adding tauntingly, 'Besides, what makes you so sure that I *do* want to buy the property; perhaps, like you, I've simply come here for a holiday...a rest and some relaxation...a couple of weeks away?'

'No!' Livvy couldn't keep the appalled denial back.

He couldn't possibly mean what he was saying; he couldn't possibly be intending to stay here, not after all the things he had said about her. He was simply doing it to torment her...to bully her. Well, she wasn't going to be bullied. She had learned enough as a teacher to be able to stand her ground.

'I don't believe you,' she told him flatly.

'Don't you?' he shrugged dismissively. 'Well, that's your choice. You aren't exactly someone I'd choose to share a house with, but...' He turned towards the door.

'You *can't* stay here,' Livvy protested.

He turned round, looking at her speculatively before telling her softly, 'Oh, but I think I can. After all, unlike you, *I* have the owner's permission to do so. Besides, I think I owe it to George to do so. To protect his interests, so to speak. Just as you are here to protect Gale's.'

'That's not true... I'm just here on holiday.'

He smiled at her, a cold, challenging, triumphant smile. 'Of course, you could always leave. In fact...'

'I'm not leaving.'

What on earth had she done? she wondered sickly, suddenly feeling oddly light-headed. She couldn't back down now, even though staying here with him was the last thing she wanted to do.

'You're not helping your cousin's marriage by doing this, you know. But then perhaps that isn't why you're here. Perhaps you're here because Gale knows that George can't sell the property while you're living in it, ostensibly a sitting tenant...'

Livvy gasped in outrage. 'That's not true! I'm simply on holiday; and besides, Gale would never do anything like that, even if...' She bit her lip. What was she doing, allowing herself to be drawn into this kind of argument with him?

She had guessed from what Gale had told her that she and George were at loggerheads over the farmhouse and that Gale was upset because George was spending so much time away from home, but she had not thought that their problems were serious enough to actually threaten their marriage.

'All Gale wants is a chance to talk to George, but that seems to be impossible while Robert Forrest... What kind of man is he, anyway?' she exploded, her emotions suddenly breaking her self-control. 'If George and Gale are having problems, then he's the one to blame. No wonder his own wife left him. I'm only surprised that he found anyone idiotic enough to marry him in the first place.'

She stopped abruptly, angry with herself. What on earth was she saying? She didn't even know the man and it was completely out of character for her to criticise someone without any real justification. It was *his* fault, this arrogant, interfering, unwanted male interloper in her life who stood watching her with those cold, dangerous eyes. *He* was bringing to the surface a side to her nature she had never even known existed.

The cold from the stone floor was beginning to strike an icy chill through her feet. All she wanted was for him to go, to leave her in peace; but he was not going to do so, she recognised, and she could not now leave herself . . . not without totally losing face and letting him know that he had got the better of her, and there was no way her feminine pride was going to allow him to do that.

He had *not* come for a holiday, no matter what he might pretend, she was sure of that, and she also suspected that he was not going to admit his real purpose to her, for no other reason than that it seemed to give him some sort of perverted pleasure to bait and torment her. Whatever his original plans had been—possibly a brief look around the farmhouse over the period of a couple of days before returning to Britain—he now intended to stay.

But he wanted *her* to leave, she recognised. Well, she wasn't going to.

She told him so, her expression dogged as she said fiercely, 'I'm not leaving and you can't make me.'

For a moment she wondered if she had gone too far. There was a look in his eyes that told her how much...how very, very much he would have liked to prove her wrong by physically picking her up and depositing her in her car if necessary.

Instead he shrugged his shoulders, powerfully broad beneath a suit far too formal for a man who claimed to be on holiday.

'That's your choice,' he told her dismissively, adding in a voice as thick and soft as cream, 'Mind you, I shouldn't have thought there would be much locally to interest a woman of your type.'

Her type? Livvy tensed. What did he mean? What was he trying to imply now? she wondered warily. Whatever it was, she knew it wasn't anything complimentary. For all its smoothness, there had been something as rough and as dangerous as jagged broken glass beneath the softness of his voice.

'What do you mean, my type?' she challenged him. Women were not *types*. They were individuals, each one of them a special and complex interweaving of a variety of traits that made them so. To suggest anything else was not merely to demean her but to demean her whole sex as well.

'You don't really need an answer, surely? But since you asked...'

From mild contempt the grey eyes changed, registering a brutal sexual speculation that rendered her powerless to do anything but stand there while he subjected her to a slow visual, sexual exploration that left her feeling numb with shock and disbelief. No man...*no* man had ever, ever looked at her like that. No man had ever dared; nor had she contemplated the idea that any man ever would. It was something so totally outside her experience, her existence, that the shock of it left her incapable not just of movement but of speech as well.

Her body knew what he had done, though, and it still managed to register its outrage and fury, her skin, her whole body flushing with such heat that she could feel it burning beneath the thin barriers of her T-shirt and wrap.

She had not realised before, she thought dizzily, that it was not just cold, and sometimes—very, very rarely now—a certain *frisson* of sensual awareness that could make her muscles tense like that and her nipples suddenly harden and push fiercely against her clothes. Anger could do it as well.

'You have no right. You know nothing about me...about my *type*,' she told him huskily, her throat thick with a mixture of shocked emotional tears and ferocious rage.

'I know as much as every other heterosexual male who's passed through the usual teenage rites of passage via the sexual games offered by more juvenile versions. The pouting-mouthed, wide-eyed, tousle-haired just-got-out-of-bed look does have a certain louche appeal to inexperienced boys.

'Fortunately one grows out of it and becomes rather more discerning with maturity.'

Livvy could hardly believe what she was hearing. The way she had just heard herself described bore so little resemblance to the truth that in any other circumstances she would have found it laughable. Her, a pouting parody of some kind of sexual bimbo? She was anything but...and as for her tousle-haired just-got-out-of-bed look... Surely he didn't think...*couldn't* think that it was with sexual motive in mind that she had staggered out of bed and come down here . . . not when she hadn't even known who her unexpected and unwanted visitor was . . .

She took a deep breath and said angrily, 'Look, Mr...' She paused, floundering, realising that she didn't even know his name.

He seemed to hesitate, to pause slightly warily before telling her curtly, reluctantly almost, 'R . . . Richard Field . . . And since it seems that we're going to be co-tenants here I suppose it might be as well to know your name. Not that I intend to make much use of it . . .'

For a moment Livvy was tempted to turn her back on him and walk away, but good manners and custom forced her to supply him with the information he had requested.

'Olivia . . . Olivia Lucy,' she told him, her voice just as curt as his had been. No need to tell him that no one other than officialdom ever referred to her by her full name, nor to say wistfully how much she sometimes wished that they would. Olivia Lucy had an elegance, a sophistication to it which was completely lacking in 'Livvy Lucy'.

'Olivia . . .' Unexpectedly his expression changed, the devastating sexual scrutiny he had subjected her to previously replaced by an equally devastating and somehow far more unsettling searching thoughtfulness that left her holding her breath, as though something of tremendous import was somehow being weighed in the balance.

When he eventually looked away from her, she derided herself angrily for her reaction. Who was he to sit in judgement on her? *She* didn't like him any more than he liked her. In fact, if anything, she probably detested him more, felt even more contempt for him than he had shown that he felt for her.

A woman of her type. She could feel herself starting to grind her teeth. Well, there was one thing she intended to make sure he did know about her, and that was that a woman of her type found a man of *his* type utterly loathsome and detestable, she decided as she turned her back on him and walked out of the room.

Just as soon as she could, she intended to telephone Gale and find out exactly what was going on, but first she needed to go back upstairs and get dressed.

She heard him coming upstairs while she was in the bathroom and automatically she grasped her towel closer to her body as she stared at the closed door.

Something about him made her feel uncomfortably and unfamiliarly aware of her femininity, her sexuality, her vulnerability, and not just because of the way he had spoken to her and looked at her; it went deeper than that, a deep-rooted feminine awareness of his maleness which seemed to add something highly charged and very dangerous to the antagonism between them. She couldn't remember ever reacting so fiercely, so passionately to any man before.

So passionately! She shivered, pulling the towel even more tightly around herself.

Her type of woman, indeed!

She grimaced as she let the towel drop, her glance drawn reluctantly to her body.

There was no truth in any of his accusations. How could there be? If her hair had been tousled it had simply been because she had just been woken up...by him. And if he had seen that unexpected—unfamiliar—hardening of her nipples, well, it wasn't her fault that he had totally misinterpreted their message.

She tensed, her face flushing as unbelievably they repeated their earlier reaction. Unwillingly she glanced down at her body, her tension increasing as she saw how flushed the areolae were, how unfamiliarly provocative the outline of her breasts.

Hurriedly she picked up the towel, wrapping it tightly round her body with fingers that shook slightly.

When she went back downstairs, fully dressed, her hair pulled back off her face in what she believed to be a neat and suitably schoolmarmish style, but which in actual fact, instead of making her look severe, simply emphasised the delicacy of her bone-structure and the femininity of her features, there was no sign of Richard Field.

When she looked through the kitchen window, she saw that his car had gone. An indiction that he had decided to do the gentlemanly thing and leave? Somehow Livvy doubted it.

However, while he *was* gone it would be a good opportunity for her to ring Gale.

CHAPTER FOUR

LIVVY dialled her cousin's number firmly, standing facing the window, determinedly keeping her fingers crossed that Gale would be in.

She was. Expelling a small sigh of relief, Livvy quickly told her what had happened. She could tell from Gale's sharp intake of breath that her news had surprised her.

'Did George tell you that he had arranged for someone to view the farmhouse?' she asked her cousin.

'No,' Gale told her.

'Gale, you must talk to him,' Livvy told her.

'Talk to him? I only wish I could,' Gale interrupted her bitterly. 'Robert has sent him away on business—again. George promised he'd ring me but he hasn't done so as yet. His secretary says she can't give me a number for him.'

Livvy could hear the anger and frustration in her cousin's voice.

Was George's desire to sell the farmhouse the cause of their marital problems, or, more worryingly, merely a symptom of some deeper conflict between them? Livvy knew her cousin well enough to know that she would not react well to any direct questioning.

Instead she said quietly, 'Gale, I feel I'm in a very invidious position. This man, this friend of George's has made it quite clear that as far as he's concerned I'm virtually trespassing, since I'm here without George's knowledge and since George is the owner of the property. In fact——'

'That's nonsense,' Gale interrupted her angrily. 'The farmhouse is as much mine as it is George's.'

'Morally perhaps, but technically...legally...'

'There's no way George would have not wanted you to stay, no matter how he and I...' She broke off and added almost pleadingly, 'Livvy, don't let this man bully you into leaving. From what you've said about him it sounds as though he's deliberately trying to drive you away. He's probably trying to push George into letting the place go at way below its market value, panicking him into an unfair deal. I know that once I've had a chance to talk to him...make him see...

'Stay there, Livvy, please.'

'If you can't get in touch with George, then surely neither can anyone else,' Livvy pointed out to her.

'No, perhaps not...apart from Robert Forrest, but I'd feel happier knowing you were there.'

Did she really have any choice? Livvy asked herself after she had replaced the receiver. And not simply because of what Gale had said.

If she left now, backed down now, wouldn't it look as though she was giving in, running away...as though she didn't have the courage to stand her ground and continue to confront him?

Her forehead puckered in thought, Livvy heard the sound of a car engine.

Tensely she watched through the window, but it wasn't a BMW that came bounding into the yard, and the man who emerged from behind the wheel of the battered truck certainly wasn't Richard Field....

This time her visitor *was* Gale's nearest neighbour, the farmer, Gustave Dubois, a short, stocky, weathered-looking man in his mid-fifties who gave Livvy's slim jeans-clad body an assessing and admiring glance as he introduced himself to her.

He had come, he told her, to make himself known to her and to deliver the small basket of provisions which *madame*, his wife, had ordered him to bring.

He had also, it transpired, come to check on the generator, which if Livvy understood him correctly was a highly temperamental piece of equipment which required very delicate and knowledgeable handling, its moodiness rather like that of a woman, the skilled touch needed to overcome its obstinacy much like that of an accomplished and knowledgeable lover.

'You will have to be firm with Monsieur Dubois,' Gale had warned her. '*Madame* keeps him on an extremely tight leash, but he's harmless really.'

She must not know despair, the farmer went on to assure her. Should a catastrophe occur and the generator break down, she only had to telephone and he would come to her aid *immédiatement*. It would in fact be his pleasure, he assured her.

He was most kind. Livvy thanked him, but perhaps if he were to show her the mere basics of how the thing worked? He had already indicated that he had brought with him a supply of fuel for it, and in doing so had managed to convey that this action had been motivated by pure gallantry and chivalry, whereas Livvy knew for a fact that Gale had a standing arrangement with him whereby not only was the generator regularly serviced, but he kept it supplied with the necessary fuel.

'Don't let him charge you anything,' Gale had warned her. 'We operate a barter system with him: the use of our land for certain services, including keeping the generator in working order, emptying the cesspit, that sort of thing.'

Show her how it worked?

He managed to look both concerned and slightly superior, as he shook his head and explained regretfully that it was not so simple a matter as that.

Had she not been made so upset and anxious by Richard Field, she would have been quite enjoying this encounter, Livvy decided. The influence of her French grandmother and holidays spent in the French countryside as a child had given her a first-hand knowledge of how the French countryman's mind worked, of the rituals to be gone through in such circumstances, but before she could say anything the farmer was turning away from her, surprise and the smallest dash of chagrin touching his face as the BMW drove into the yard.

As Richard Field got out of the car and studied them with frowning concentration, he said quickly to Livvy, 'Ah, I hadn't realised. Madame Gale did not say that you would be accompanied by your husband...'

'He is not my husband...' Livvy denied immediately as Richard Field walked over to join them.

She could tell from his expression that he had heard her, although she didn't realise the full significance of either his smile or her own comment until later.

In fact she was too incensed to be aware of anything beyond the fact that Monsieur Dubois, upon seeing Richard Field, had turned his back on her and was now explaining to him in rapid French just what had brought him to the farm.

It was pointless reminding herself that here in the countryside the old hierarchy still existed and that Monsieur Dubois could have no idea of how much pleasure it would be giving Richard Field that she was being dismissed as a mere woman while the farmer gave Richard a graphic and far more detailed description than he had given her of the complexities and temperament of the generator.

As she watched Richard listening quietly, without taking up any of the subtle male challenge the farmer was giving him as he commented on how no one could expect *monsieur*, a stranger to these parts, and to the generator in particular, to be able to deal competently with its temperamentality, Livvy felt a distinct deepening of her own apprehension.

The arrogance and insensitivity he had shown her evidently cloaked a far more subtle awareness of how to deal with people...and of how to manipulate them. Was that what he had been doing with her earlier... *trying* to provoke the kind of reaction from her which would send her from the farmhouse in a headlong flight of fury and resentment, thus leaving him in sole possession?

If *monsieur* insisted, he would certainly show him how the generator worked, Gustave Dubois was agreeing, managing to combine a verbal willingness to please with a strong note of doubt as to his would-be pupil's abilities.

As they started to walk towards the outbuildings, Livvy hurried to join them. She was not going to allow Richard Field any advantage over her, even if the total sum of her practical knowledge of anything electrical was limited to an ability to change a fuse and wire up a plug.

It was the farmer who defeated her, pausing just as they entered the outbuildings to turn round and suggest

to her that a cup of coffee or, better still, a glass of wine
would be very much welcomed.

Livvy's face burned as she sensed Richard Field's
contempt and triumph, but there was nothing she could
do. Firmly refusing to look at Richard Field and allow
him to see her chagrin, she marched over to where the
farmer had left the basket of provisions from his wife.
Picking it up, she carried it into the kitchen, frowning
as she glanced towards the cold range.

She suspected that, skilled as he might be with the
generator, Monsieur Dubois would consider the workings
of the range to be a female rather than a male area of
knowledge.

'Watch the range,' Gale had warned her. 'If the wind's
in the wrong direction when you light it, it sulks and
smokes dreadfully.'

She had no real need to light it, Livvy told herself;
after all, there was a stove, of sorts; but without its
warmth, without its life, the kitchen felt dead and empty,
and besides, if she busied herself with lighting it, it would
give her a perfect excuse for not having to provide the
two men with a drink. Not that she would have objected
to providing the *farmer* with one, but when it came to
Richard Field... She was, she discovered, grinding her
teeth at the thought of doing anything, anything at all
to allow him to believe that she was subservient to
him... in any way.

Half an hour later, hot and grubby, she grinned with
triumph as she opened the fire door of the range to see
the comforting glow of a well-established fire.

Lighting it was one thing, she reminded herself ruefully, as she closed the door, cooking on it with any
degree of success was quite another.

She remembered the long summer holidays spent with a distant relative of her grandmother's in Normandy, and the gloom which had befallen the whole household when Grandmère, who ruled the kitchen and the range, broke her arm.

Her daughter-in-law, well into her forties, with almost grown-up children of her own, had broken down in tears over the soup, and in the end Grandmère had had to give instructions as to how the range had to be coaxed and bullied into providing the family with the meals it was used to.

Well, *she* was not going to be providing any family with meals, Livvy reassured herself as she wiped the top of the range clear of dust and returned to the sink to wash her grimy hands.

She wondered how long it would be before Richard Field grew tired of the game he was playing with her and decided to leave. Not too long, she hoped. And in the meantime she would just have to learn to live with his unwanted presence, for Gale's sake.

How could George behave so unkindly, so unfairly? It was totally unlike him. Livvy's tender heart ached for her cousin and his children.

She saw the two men coming back across the yard, and frowned as she saw the friendly, almost approving way the farmer clapped Richard on the back before shaking his head and walking over to his truck. Something Richard Field had said or done had obviously impressed the farmer and earned his respect.

It was several minutes after the farmer had left before Richard came into the kitchen, and when he did he was carrying a box of provisions.

Even from where she stood, Livvy could smell the rich scent of the fresh baked bread he had bought, and her mouth started to water. She had still not had her breakfast, although it was almost lunchtime.

She had made herself a cup of coffee...instant, but at least it was a drink; but now, as she smelled the fresh bread, she remembered resentfully how, before Richard Field had arrived to spoil everything, she had planned to drive into the local town and buy croissants for her breakfast.

'You've lit the range.'

She saw him frown and walk over to check, almost as though he didn't believe it, and Livvy felt a small spurt of satisfaction that she had managed to throw him a little. No doubt in his book women of her *type* had only one set of skills...the sort learned and honed in a wide variety of different men's beds.

'Monsieur Dubois sends his apologies for not coming in to say goodbye,' he told her. 'I suspect he is afraid that *madame* would not approve of him consorting with a fallen woman, one so free with her favours that she openly admits she is not married to her lover.'

Livvy stared at him, her normal calm deserting her as she confronted him, shock and fury two equally powerful forces within her as she demanded fiercely, 'What have you said to him? What lies have you told him? He *knows* that I'm Gale's cousin. Gale telephoned...'

'*I* have said nothing,' he interrupted her, unkind relish darkening in his eyes as he told her, 'You yourself were the one who told him that I was not your husband.'

'Not my husband, and not my lover either... I...'

'Monsieur Dubois does not see it that way. In his view, when two people, a man and a woman, choose to spend time together at a secluded, remote farmhouse deep in the countryside, there can be only one reason for their doing so.'

'But it's not true,' Livvy burst out when the significance of his taunting comment had finally sunk in. 'You should have told him ... explained ...'

'I did try, but he seemed to think that I was merely attempting to protect your honour. It seems that I am not alone in recognising you for what you are, *chérie*.'

His insulting use of that small word of supposed endearment was the last straw; Livvy crossed the distance that separated them, her face flushed with heat, an anger she had never ever experienced before overwhelming her.

'You have no idea of what I am,' she denied furiously. 'And nor will you ever know. You and I ... *lovers*.' She flashed him a look of concentrated loathing and fury, desperately trying to control the small quiver of her tightly closed mouth. 'Never, never would I let someone like you touch me.' She gave a small shudder, her body involuntarily reinforcing the passion in her words, and subconsciously registering her revulsion at her earlier inexplicable sensual awareness of him.

She turned to move away from him, but he moved first, her body going rigid with shock as he took hold of her.

As though somehow she herself was distanced from it, her brain separated somehow from her body, she was aware of registering the pressure with which he was gripping her upper arms; the anger that emanated from him, surrounding him—engulfing her with an almost physical heat.

She had never seen a man so angry before, and had certainly never been responsible for that anger: a dangerous, sexual anger that made his eyes glitter with such brilliance and fierceness that she had to look away from him, her body starting to tremble with humiliating female vulnerability and reaction as she recognised her danger.

Her still lips struggled to form the word 'no' just as she tried to free herself from him, but one brief, despairing look into his implacable face told her that there was going to be no mercy.

She had known right from the start what he had intended to do, but, in the handful of seconds which elapsed between his taking hold of her and giving vent to the fury she had aroused in him by punishing her with the hard pressure of his mouth, a part of her had still refused to accept that he would actually do it, that he would actually take her mouth in that savage, punishing parody of a kiss.

She tried to stop him, to turn her head away, but he anticipated her, releasing one of her arms to slide his hand along her jaw, holding her head still, making her completely vulnerable to him.

She stared at him wide-eyed, willing him to release her, her body, her mouth frozen with shock, but he refused to be quelled, and something in the hot, male glitter of his eyes made her own burn with the threat of tears so that she had to close them to defend herself.

Immediately, she wished she hadn't done so. With her eyes closed, she was acutely conscious of his hand against her skin, the strength, the power, the heat of his fingers.

She shivered as she felt them stroking against her skin, a wave of heat and panic engulfing her as she realised what had caused that tiny physical reaction.

She couldn't possibly be aroused by him. It was just anger...rage...combined with her fear that was making her body tremble and start to ache. It couldn't possibly have anything to do with the way his fingertips were slowly caressing her throat, nor the fact that he had now released her other arm and was holding her unforgivably close to his body, binding her against him with the pressure of the arm he had wrapped around her, holding her so close that she could feel his heart beating, savagely uneven, thudding out a primitive message of male anger, male arousal...a male adrenalin-induced need to meet the challenge she had so dangerously flung down between them.

Her lips felt soft, swollen, vulnerable to the deliberately sensual assault of his. He wasn't just expressing his anger, she recognised, he was trying to *arouse* her as well...to punish her and taunt her by calling her a liar.

She tried desperately not to react, not to respond, but she could feel herself losing control, losing the ability to think and fight, giving in to the jolting surge of desire overpowering her, her mouth softening, opening, clinging, her breath escaping on a soft, aching sigh of pleasure as he took advantage of her weakness, sliding his tongue between her parted lips, stroking and caressing them until she felt dizzy, light-headed, incapable of anything other than giving in to him.

Against her body she could feel the unfamiliar shape and hardness of his, the tautness of his muscles, the strength and power which they sheathed.

His heartbeat was rough and heavy now, the heat coming off his skin engulfing her, the scent of him drugging her like an opiate.

She tried to fight it, to open her eyes, to break the spell he seemed to have cast over her, but her eyelids felt too heavy, the demand of his mouth too strong. She could feel herself starting to tremble as the ache inside her grew, and she knew that he could feel it too. She felt him check and then heard him make a small explosive sound against her mouth. His hand moved up over her body, cupping her breast, finding the taut peak of her nipple, caressing it.

She made a small anguished sound of shocked pleasure, her eyes opening wide, brilliant with shock and arousal as she look straight up into his.

His hand stilled on her body, his expression suddenly changing, becoming hard and cold. He released her so unexpectedly that she half stumbled, her face flushing with mortification as the realisation of what had happened flooded over her.

'As I said,' he told her contemptuously as he studied her, 'I know your type.'

And then, without another word or look, he walked past her, opened the door and went out into the yard.

Livvy couldn't move. Her body felt stiff and cold, every joint and muscle ached, but the pain she was suffering physically was nothing compared with her mental anguish, her shock and self-revulsion.

What on earth had come over her? *Why* had she let him humiliate her like that? She was not sexually promiscuous, not easily aroused to physical desire, not someone who normally allowed herself to get out of control.

She started to shake. She felt sick with self-revulsion and shame. Close to tears, she went upstairs.

Why on earth had she let him do that to her? Why on earth had she been stupid enough to throw down that idiotic challenge in the first place?

If she hadn't given Gale her word that she would stay, she would be packing her things right now, ready to admit defeat rather than have to face him again and to see in his eyes, in his manner towards her, how much he was relishing his victory over her. But she had given Gale her promise, and the situation her cousin was in was of far more importance than her own feelings.

She froze as she heard footsteps on the stairs, unable to relax properly even when they went past her room and she heard the opening and then the closing of the door of the bedroom he had decided to occupy.

It made no difference telling herself that she had not been the only one to be aroused; that he too... In fact it had just the opposite effect, causing her to shudder deeply with self-disgust as she fought to deny her awareness of how at the time, in his arms, held close against his body, the primitive female core of her had actually relished the hard, aroused feel of him against her.

Since she couldn't escape from him by running away, the only alternative left to her was to ignore him, to brazen it out and pretend that she was totally unaffected by what had happened, to behave not just as though she was totally unaware of his contempt, but also totally indifferent to it.

To behave, in effect, as the sort of woman he claimed he knew her to be would behave.

What, after all, was worse? Which would make her more vulnerable... allowing him to believe that she was a sexual opportunist who responded to her body's desire for sex with whatever man happened to be available, or letting him guess the truth, that her reaction to him, the way she had behaved in his arms, the response she had felt, was so far outside her normal experience that she had been totally overwhelmed by it, unable to either control it or defend herself against it?

She tensed as she heard him going back downstairs, relaxing only when she heard the slam of his car door and then the sound of the engine.

He had gone out. Thank goodness. If only he might *never* come back.

Who knew, perhaps by fulfilling Richard Field's scathing description of what she was, she might not only be able to conceal from him how vulnerable he made her feel, but perhaps cause him such irritation and revulsion that he might actually leave?

His departure would not necessarily prevent George from finding another buyer for the farmhouse, but it would at least give Gale some extra time to sort things out with her husband.

Attack was supposed to be the best form of defence, she reminded herself, so instead of cowering nervously and becoming filled with humiliation, the next time Richard Field chose to denigrate her verbally—or physically—perhaps she ought to show him just how much a 'woman of a certain type' she could be.

He had used those words deliberately to humiliate her. Well, now perhaps she ought to think about finding a way of using them against him.

CHAPTER FIVE

LIVVY paced restlessly round the kitchen. Richard Field had been gone for almost an hour. Where was he? When would he be back...?

She stopped abruptly. Why should *she* concern herself with him? Wasn't it far more sensible simply to carry on with her plans as though he had never arrived to upset and unnerve her?

There was that long list of chores Gale had given her for a start, and Monsieur Dubois had left before she had had an opportunity to ask him about the gas supply to the cooker and fridge.

She had no idea how much or how little might be left in the existing containers, but common sense told her that it would be a good idea not only to have a reserve supply but also to know that she was able to change over the canisters when necessary. They looked heavy, and she suspected that the betraying signs of rust on the connections would mean that a certain amount of brute force might be necessary to release an empty container and replace it with a fresh one.

No doubt, along with the generator, the farmer had deemed this a male area of skill and knowledge, but she did not want to be left in a position where she was dependent on Richard Field, not only for lighting and hot water, but for cooking as well...

She had stoked the range, unpacked and put away her clothes and the provisions, cleaned the kitchen and ex-

66

plored the rest of the house, apart from the bedroom which Richard Field had commandeered.

As Gale had rightly said, the farmhouse, while structurally sound, needed a considerable amount of work doing on it.

'No way will that one antiquated bathroom be enough,' she had told Livvy, 'especially if we invite friends down. I've told George we'll need at least two extra bathrooms, one for us, one for guests, and possibly a shower-room as well.'

'I've spoken to the local builder—he's Monsieur Dubois' cousin. Of course, he pretended at first that he would be too busy to do anything for months, but they all try that on... I want you to go and see him, Livvy, and remind him that I want work started on the alterations this summer. I've given you a list of the bathroom fittings and the sanitaryware. When you order it, make sure the plumber gives you a firm delivery date...'

It was a great pity that Gale herself couldn't have been here, Livvy reflected feelingly. With her cousin to contend with, Richard Field would have found himself in a very different situation indeed.

Since she was here for the whole summer, she did not really need to tackle the list of instructions Gale had given her immediately, but she suspected that her cousin would expect her to deal with them with the same gusto and determination which she herself would have exhibited, and besides, she felt too tense and on edge to relax properly and too off balance still to want to be here when Richard Field got back.

Gale, typically well organised, had supplied her with maps and even given her a list of places of local interest, the hill town of Rocamadour, the caves and underground lake aptly named River Styx of Gouffre de Padirac. She had been looking forward to exploring the region, to enjoying its richly wooded countryside and famous rivers; she had been looking forward to peace and solitude, to an opportunity to replenish her spiritual and mental resources. Now...

Now she was a seething, agitated mass of jangling nerves and tensions.

She drove first to the farm, to thank Madame Dubois for her kind welcoming gift and to submit herself to the older woman's appraisal and inspection.

It would have been an affront to *madame* were she not the first to be able to report on the new visitor.

Livvy's French ancestry, already known to *madame*, was re-examined and discussed, *madame*'s probing enquiries as to the reasons for Gale's and the children's non-appearance gently sidestepped, and Livvy was on the point of leaving when *madame* commented to her that *monsieur*, her friend, also spoke excellent French.

Did he too have the benefit of French blood in his veins? *madame* asked her.

Livvy checked. It was obvious that Monsieur Dubois had told his wife that they were lovers, and Livvy had the frustrating conviction that, no matter how much she tried to tell the older woman the truth, she would not be able to convince her.

The countryperson's mind was an earthy one, Livvy knew that, but nevertheless it galled that already in the minds of local people she was seen as Richard Field's lover.

Resisting the impulse to tell *madame* that she neither knew nor cared what Richard Field's ancestry was, she took her leave of her.

Her next port of call was the home of Monsieur Dubois' cousin, the builder. As Livvy had expected, he was out, but his wife made her welcome, listening while Livvy explained her mission.

Armand, her husband, had only the previous day mentioned the work he had promised to do for *madame*, her cousin, she told Livvy.

From the village, Livvy drove on to the local market town, not because she was reluctant to return to the farmhouse—and potentially Richard Field, she assured herself—but she was after all supposed to be on holiday, enjoying herself and relaxing, and she certainly could not do that with such an antagonistic, overbearing, judgemental and totally impossible man about.

The market town was small and pretty, surrounded by heavily wooded countryside, its dominating architectural feature the stone bridge spanning the river. As she drove across it, she saw half a dozen men fishing on its banks. George was a keen fisherman, part of the reason he and Gale had opted to buy the farmhouse. But now it seemed there would be little chance of her cousin and her husband spending long family summer holidays here.

Sadly, Livvy parked her car, a fresh anger stirring against Richard Field for adding to the stress Gale must already be under. From his comments, it was obvious that he was well aware of the discord between Gale and George. As George's friend, he should be advising him to repair the damage to his marriage, not seeking to take advantage of the situation by trying to push through an underhand deal to buy the farmhouse.

However, from the opinions he had expressed to her, it was obvious just how he looked upon her sex, Livvy acknowledged, and as she headed towards the small market square her face burned as she recalled his comments to her and how he had reacted when she . . .

She stopped walking, her body tensing as she tried to reject the sharp thrill of sensation quivering through her.

She was not really sexually responsive to him, she denied. That had just been a momentary aberration, a brief heartbeat of misjudgement by her bemused senses. It meant nothing, and if just now, remembering, she had for one unnerving second actually felt her body quiver into unexpected awareness, her mouth soften as though it could actually physically recall the intense sensuality of his kiss, then that meant nothing too.

The small town was very quiet. Good French housewives did their shopping early in the day, when things were still fresh and choice abundant. Now the town drowsed in the later afternoon sunshine, the small group of men seated outside the bar on the edge of the square watching Livvy with admiring interest as she crossed their line of vision.

Tempted by the cool shade promised by a narrow alleyway leading off the square, Livvy walked down it, pausing outside a small bookshop.

In England she had not given much thought to how she would occupy her evenings; she had plenty of work to do preparing things for the new school term; she had her radio and tapes, and had assumed that, after long, lazy days spent exploring the countryside, she would be only too glad to have some early nights.

That, though, had been before she had discovered that she would be sharing the farmhouse with Richard Field. Somehow she could not imagine herself feeling relaxed enough to do that while he was around.

She would need something to occupy her time, to put a safe, uncrossable distance between them. She went into the bookshop, emerging over half an hour later, after an enjoyable conversation with the proprietress, carrying a parcel which contained the two novels she had bought.

Yes, they should keep her well and truly occupied for the next few evenings, and make it clear to a certain wrong-headed male that she was quite definitely not interested in him. All she had to do was to sit tight and wait for him to leave. He couldn't be planning to stay very long—could he?

As she drove back to the farmhouse, the closer she got to her destination, the slower she was driving, Livvy recognised. What was wrong with her? She wasn't afraid of him, was she?

Not afraid, but his assessment of her, his denunciation of her, however wildly wrong they might have been, had left her feeling vulnerable as well as angry.

Was it that, or was it that shatteringly unexpected brief reaction to him which was disturbing her?

Uncomfortable with her thoughts, Livvy drove into the farmyard and discovered to her relief that there was no sign of the BMW.

Garaging her own car in one of the large empty buildings, she gathered up her purchases and headed for the house, stopping in surprise when she saw the small, thin cat waiting hopefully by the door.

Automatically she bent down to stroke it, smiling as it responded with a loud purr, weaving itself round her legs.

Although its tabby coat was glossy, its body was thin, the amber eyes pleadingly hopeful as Livvy reached into her handbag for her keys. It had probably come from one of the local farms, she acknowledged, as she opened the door and it followed her inside, and just as probably wasn't likely to be missed... It had the lean outline of a farmyard hunter rather than a domestic pet, although it seemed to have all the instincts of the latter, from the way it had greeted her and was now making straight for the warmth of the range.

She hadn't the heart to put it back outside, and before very long Livvy discovered that she was responding with shameful weakness to the silent plea in the amber eyes, pouring it a saucer of milk and rooting through her provisions until she came across a tin of sardines.

Quelling her conscience by telling herself that, as a farm cat, it would probably be a good mouser, she tried not to listen to the sharp voice of her conscience warning her that Gale might not be too pleased about her new house guest.

An hour later, as she sat down to enjoy the omelette she had just made and drink the glass of clean, sharp-tasting if a little rough local wine she had bought, she reflected that if it had not been for Richard Field's unwanted presence life would be not very far short of perfect.

The kitchen warmed by the range and scented with the rich smell of her cooking, the cat half sleeping, half purring by the fire in front of her; the familiar comforting and yet exciting ambience of a French country kitchen; in the half-light of dusk, stirring memories of happy childhood holidays in Brittany, all combined to make her aware of how much tension she had been under lately, how little time she had had for enjoying this kind of simple pleasure and relaxation.

And if she accepted the assistant headship, there would be even less time. She had gone into teaching because she wanted to teach, and the dilemma she now found herself facing depressed her.

Of course she wanted to progress—who wouldn't? But as a teacher, not an administrative manager.

She wondered if Gale had had any success in getting in touch with George. She must phone her. She was frowning as she carried her empty plate and glass over to the sink. Richard Field still hadn't returned. Where was he?

It irked her that she should be so preoccupied with him. It was just because he had made her so angry, she told herself as she washed the things she had used.

Gale and George were going to have to spend a good deal of money if they were to achieve all the improvements Gale wanted, Livvy reflected as she dialled her cousin's telephone number. In Gale's shoes, she wasn't sure she would want to go ahead with putting the work in hand in view of the problems she and George were facing, but Gale had been adamant when she spoke to her that she was not going to let what she had described as George's foolishness change her plans.

As Livvy waited for her cousin to answer her call, she frowned unhappily. It upset her to know that her cousin was having matrimonial problems, for the children's sakes as well as for Gale's and George's. For George actually to take steps to sell the farmhouse without telling Gale was the last thing she would have expected him to do.

Gale wasn't answering the phone; she must be out. Livvy replaced the receiver and removed the list of chores

Gale had given her from her handbag, placing it on the table.

While she was studying it, the cat jumped up on to her knee, miaowing plaintively. Laughing, Livvy stroked her. The cat responded with a loud purr and settled herself comfortably on Livvy's lap.

'Oh, no, you don't,' Livvy told her. 'I'm going upstairs to have a shower and an early night. You, I'm afraid, are going to have to go out...'

The cat purred more loudly. Perhaps in the morning she would be gone, back from wherever she had come from, Livvy reflected. If so, she would miss her; there was something comforting about her presence, something reassuring. She stood up with the cat in her arms and then froze as she heard the sound of a car's engine and saw its headlights as it turned into the yard.

Richard Field was back. Only now did Livvy acknowledge how much a part of her had been hoping that he had changed his mind...done the decent thing and decided to leave.

She wasn't the kind of person who enjoyed confrontation or arguments, but she wouldn't, couldn't let him bully her into giving way to him.

Still holding the cat, she waited for him to appear, watching as the door-handle turned and the door itself opened inwards.

For a moment, as he saw her, he looked almost shocked, and then he demanded grimly, 'Hasn't anyone warned you about the dangers of leaving doors unlocked? Anyone could have walked in. Or was that perhaps what you were waiting for?' he added softly, his mouth curling into a cynical, derogatory smile. 'I don't suppose a woman like you can go very long without sex. Who is it this time? Another casual pick-up like the one at the *auberge*?'

Livvy clutched the cat tightly, ignoring the small protesting sound it made, tension holding her body stiffly upright, her mind flinching from his words as though they were actual physical blows, but she refused to let him see how much his accusations and attitude had affected her.

She was not even going to dignify them by denying them. She had no need to prove anything to him, defend herself from remarks which all those who knew her would have found laughably absurd. It was on the tip of her tongue to tell him that, contrary to what he had imagined, she had not invited those unwanted attentions—and to add that it was no thanks to him that she had escaped being raped.

In her arms, the cat gave a protesting miaow and wriggled.

Immediately he focused on it, frowning.

'Where did that come from?' he demanded.

'I found her outside. Not that it's any business of yours,' Livvy told him furiously.

He was looking at her, his eyes full of contempt and a brilliant, dangerous anger. It was almost as though he wanted her to challenge him, to provoke him, Livvy recognised, swallowing on her reaction to him.

'You realise that it's probably covered you in fleas?' he told her.

Livvy refused to respond. What did he think she was? The kind of silly idiot who would immediately throw the cat to the floor in horror? Nevertheless, she made a mental note to buy some flea powder when she next went shopping.

Ignoring his comment, she walked towards the door, still carrying the cat in her arms.

His terse, 'Where are you going?' checked her just as she reached it, and this time as she turned round to face him she made no attempt to hide her anger. Her eyes were brilliant with it, her whole body registering her independence and resentment.

'I'm putting the cat out for the night, before I go to bed. Not that it's any business of yours,' she told him fiercely.

'Going to bed? At this time?' His eyebrows rose. 'Somehow you don't strike me as the early-night-with-a-good-book type.'

'The reason I'm going to bed early is because I can't bear the thought of having to spend any more time than I have to in *your* company.'

She opened the door, put the cat down and closed her eyes, trying to steady herself. Her car was parked only yards away and for a moment she was achingly tempted to get in it and simply drive away. But how could she do that? She had promised Gale she would stay, and besides, why should she allow a man like that to bully and manipulate her? And that was what he was doing. He was probably hoping she would leave, already gloating mentally over his victory over her.

Taking deep, steady breaths of fresh air, she turned round and walked back into the kitchen.

As she walked past him, Livvy saw that he was studying the list she had left on the kitchen table. Lifting his head, he looked at her, his eyes cold and cynical.

'I see that despite the fact that Gale doesn't seem to want George's company, she isn't averse to spending his money. How like a woman.'

'That isn't true,' Livvy defended her cousin hotly. 'George is the one who...' She caught herself up abruptly. She wasn't going to discuss her cousin's marriage with him.

'Gale made those plans for the farmhouse last year...'

'When she must have known that George had already over-extended himself to buy this place. No wonder the poor devil is...' He stopped abruptly while Livvy stared at him, her own feelings pushed to one side as she wondered how he came to know so much about George's financial affairs. George had never struck her as the kind of man to confide in other members of his sex. Come to think of it, a man like Richard Field was the very last kind of man she would have imagined someone like George having as a close friend. They were so completely opposite. George, the devoted, mild-tempered, placid husband and father, Richard Field, so openly contemptuous of her sex, and so very obviously neither mild nor placid.

And at the back of her mind, although she fought to acknowledge it, was an awareness of the greatest difference between them: George was her cousin's husband and she knew Gale loved him, but there was no way that even her cousin could claim that George possessed one-tenth of the intense male sexuality that Richard Field had in such abundance.

'Did your cousin even think of the financial burden she was forcing on him when she overruled him and insisted on buying this place?'

'Gale wanted the farmhouse so that they could all come here and relax,' Livvy protested, but nevertheless she was biting her bottom lip, remembering how often in the past other members of the family had criticised

Gale for her domineering ways, and for the manner in which she often steamrollered over any opposition to her wishes.

Gale would never knowingly do anything to hurt George, Livvy was sure, but perhaps unknowingly... She caught herself up... What was she doing, allowing him to sway her judgement, to...?

Across the table from her he gave a harsh snort of derision.

'For them all to enjoy? Or for her to brag about to her friends...'

'She wanted to be able to get George to take a proper holiday,' Livvy interrupted furiously. 'She wanted to get him away from that monster of a boss of his who treats him like a slave, making him work virtually twenty-four hours a day. If there are any problems to Gale and George's marriage, then he's the one who's caused them with his impossible demands on George, not Gale... Gale and George were perfectly happily married until he took over the company...'

Livvy stopped. She was breathing hard, her face flushed, her temper high. She flicked a look in Richard Field's direction.

His face was shadowed and unreadable, his body still.

Something about his silence, his stillness goaded Livvy on, rushing her into impetuous, angry speech as she added contemptuously,

'No wonder his own marriage ended in divorce. I wouldn't be surprised if he actually *wanted* to break up George and Gale's marriage, if he was actually deliberately...'

'You don't know what the hell you're talking about.'

Livvy tensed, blinking nervously. Something she had said had obviously touched a raw nerve. She had never seen him looking so angry, not even before when he had... She shivered and backed nervously away from the table. If he should try to take hold of her again, to punish her with a repeat performance... This time he wouldn't find her such an easy victim; this time she would be prepared, on her guard; this time she would be able to withstand the fierce intensity of his sexuality, meeting it with icy coldness, letting him know how she truly felt about him, how...

'If your cousin really wants to find an explanation for the breakdown of her marriage, she should look to her own behaviour and not try to blame it on someone else...'

The flat, dead tone of his voice made Livvy focus on him; his reaction was so very different from the charged, intense response she had had from him earlier that it took her several seconds to recognise that she had nothing to fear; that he was not going to reach for her and take hold of her, subjecting her to the kind of physical domination and punishment he had inflicted on her before.

'I am not going to discuss my cousin's marriage with you,' she told him. 'Your criticism of Gale is unfair and ill-judged, but then...'

She paused, recognising that there was little point in telling him that he was as wrong about Gale as he had been about her. The man plainly had a bias against the female sex, despite the fact that the aura of intense, raw sexuality which surrounded him must surely attract women to him like moths to a flame.

'Yes?' he prompted broodingly, watching her with a concentration that made her shiver again. 'But then what...?'

Livvy shook her head. What was the point in entangling herself in another confrontation with him? She picked up her parcel of books off the table and turned away from him.

It was barely nine o'clock, and yet her body ached as though she had been up far longer and worked much harder, Livvy recognised as she showered tiredly. Her muscle-tension was no doubt the result of the strain Richard Field's presence was imposing on her.

She was beginning to regret giving Gale her promise to stay, and yet there was also a small, stubborn part of her that would have been reluctant to retreat and leave Richard Field in victorious possession of the day—and the farmhouse.

It had been unfair of him to make those accusations against Gale. After all, what did *he* know of her? Gale had known nothing about him... Which meant that he could only have drawn his conclusions about her from things George had said to him.

Livvy paused as she got out of the shower, frowning as she turned this knowledge over in her mind, ignoring the damp, naked state of her body as she worried at her thoughts.

Used to living on her own and the privacy of her small home, where she was accustomed to padding naked from her bathroom to her bedroom, it had never occurred to Livvy to lock the bathroom door.

In fact she was so disturbed by the issues raised by her thoughts that, when the bathroom door first opened and Richard Field walked in, she simply stared at him blankly until he drawled unkindly, 'If this is meant to be some kind of invitation, then the answer is no...'

Flushing hotly, Livvy reached for her towel, wrapping it quickly round her naked body, outrage battling with embarrassment.

'You had no right to walk in here without knocking,' she protested huskily.

'You should have locked the door.'

'If I'd known you were going to come creeping in here like a...like a voyeur, I would have done,' she retaliated.

She felt flustered and angry, thrown on the defensive and still embarrassed. Surely he *must* have realised as he opened the door that she was in here... Why hadn't he simply closed it again and gone tactfully away?

Because he just wasn't that kind of man, she reflected bitterly, because he was enjoying goading and humiliating her. She could just imagine how she would have felt had their positions been reversed; no way would she simply have stood there and stared, the way he had been staring at her...

It was on the tip of her tongue to resort to childhood and ask what was wrong, hadn't he seen a naked woman before? But she suspected that to do so would be very dangerous indeed, and highly provocative as well.

She could see already that she had angered him by her earlier accusation. He confirmed it as he leaned towards her, blocking her exit, asking her softly, 'What is it exactly you're trying to do? I've already told you I'm not interested. Still, I'll give it to you...you don't give up easily. What is it? Does the thought of having sex with a man whom you know despises you excite you so much that it overcomes the potential humiliation of being rejected, or is it just that you're so desperate for sex that you don't care *who* you have it with?'

Livvy gave a small, choked gasp of shocked fury. There were a hundred things she wanted to say, denials she wanted to make, feelings she wanted to give vent to, but stronger than any one of them was her need to escape from him and from the humiliation scalding her.

Before she had met him, she would have laughed in disbelief at the idea of any man saying such things to her. She was simply not that kind of woman. She was quite reticent and even a little remote with the opposite sex, and she had certainly never, ever felt the remotest need to behave in any of the ways he was suggesting.

She could feel her legs starting to tremble and she was afraid that if she didn't get away from him soon she would disgrace herself completely by either fainting or bursting into tears.

Her heart was pounding as though she had run a mile; she felt sick, tense and very, very vulnerable.

He moved slightly away from the door and she took her chance, almost running through it as she told him through gritted teeth, '*You* were the one who came barging in here. I did *not* invite you. If one of us is looking for sex, it certainly isn't me...'

She shot past him and into her bedroom without allowing him to make any response and then stood leaning against the door while her body trembled with shocked reaction.

Beneath her towel she could feel the too-fast beat of her heart—and the taut stiffness of her nipples.

CHAPTER SIX

LIVVY didn't sleep well. Her dreams were disturbed by vague images of a tall, dark-haired, hard-mouthed man who pursued her relentlessly, threatening her in some nerve-jarring, insubstantial manner that brought her abruptly out of her sleep, her mouth dry and her heart pounding heavily.

The moonlight streaming into her room alerted her to the fact that she had forgotten to close the curtains. She got up and padded quietly across to the window, halting tensely as she looked down into the yard and saw the solitary, motionless figure of Richard Field.

He was standing with his back to her, hands thrust deep in his pockets, something about his stance, its tension and remoteness making her pause instead of turning quickly away.

Alone in the moonlit yard, he seemed a different man from the one who had behaved so mercilessly to her earlier, less aggressive and antagonistic, the power and harshness she had sensed so strongly in him earlier muted.

As she watched, the cat she had fed earlier suddenly appeared, padding towards him, winding herself lovingly around his ankles. Livvy stiffened, half expecting him to push the cat away, but to her surprise instead he bent down and stroked her. He was talking to her, she recognised, and although she was too far away to hear

what he was saying, she could still see the softly rueful
smile which curved his mouth.

The sight of him exhibiting such a totally unexpected
show of tenderness and humanity made her eyes sting
suddenly with tears.

Fiercely blinking them away, she stepped back from
the window.

'Sentimental idiot,' she derided herself as she hurried
back to bed. Just because he had stroked the cat, that
didn't change anything. It didn't change him, nor his
attitude towards her. Just because for a second he had
seemed human, and not just human but someone vulnerable and alone as well, that did not give her over-
susceptible emotions an excuse to start reacting so
treacherously.

He was still the same man who had uttered those
dreadful insults, who had treated her so unforgivably... who was plotting with George to buy the
farmhouse behind Gale's back.

He had insulted her, humiliated her, made it all too
plain what he thought of her, and yet, despite all that,
some treacherous female part of her still remained very
aware of him. Too aware.

She shivered as she got back into bed and pulled the
bedclothes firmly over her head.

'No dreams this time,' she warned her subconscious.
'It's bad enough having to put up with him when I'm
awake. I'd like my sleep to be relaxing and free of
Richard Field, if you please...'

It must have worked, because when Livvy woke up in
the morning and saw the clear blue sky outside, she
rubbed her eyes in disbelief, grinning with pleasure as

she remembered where she was. Six whole lovely, uninterrupted weeks in this peaceful, pastoral paradise.
Bliss... And then abruptly she remembered that this
particular paradise had its own very definite serpent in
the large and unfriendly form of Richard Field.

Well, she wasn't going to let him spoil her holiday,
Livvy told herself firmly, and who knew, she decided
optimistically, perhaps this morning he might have
changed his mind, come to his senses and realised how
unfair, how dishonest really his and George's plans were,
and decided to leave?

It was, after all, what any sane, responsible person
would decide to do, wasn't it?

Remembering what had happened the previous
evening, Livvy was very careful to check the landing and
to lock the bathroom door while she had showered and
washed her hair.

Her optimistic mood continued when she went downstairs and found that she had the kitchen to herself.

Since she had not been able to shop properly yet, she
would have to make do with cereal and coffee for her
breakfast, but she could at least eat outside and enjoy
the early morning warmth of the sunshine.

At present the yard wasn't a particularly prepos-
sessing place, but it didn't take much imagination to
transform it mentally with the addition of terracotta pots
full of tumbling flowers, a wistaria perhaps framing the
untidy collection of outbuildings, some weathered
wooden seats padded with a collection of pretty cotton
cushions in bright summer colours. Smiling to herself,
Livvy let her imagination run riot.

A loud purring noise close at hand warned her that she was no longer alone. She laughed as she opened her eyes and bent down to greet her visitor.

Yes, Livvy decided as the cat jumped up on to her knee and settled happily there, purring, she had been silly yesterday to let Richard Field get to her; the best thing, the most sensible thing for her to do was simply to ignore him, to pretend he just did not exist. Today for instance, instead of thinking about him, worrying about when he might appear and what he might say or do, she was simply going to concentrate on enjoying herself and carrying out all the happy plans she had made before she left England.

What she was not going to do was to allow him to bully or blackmail her into leaving, nor was she going to let him spoil her holiday.

'No way,' she told the cat firmly as she determinedly picked up the guidebook she had brought outside with her and opened it.

Since she needed to shop, today would be a good opportunity to drive into Beaulieu and seek out the bathroom fittings shop Gale had detailed on her list.

Once she had completed that task, she would then indulge herself with something a little more to her liking. Not the trip to the caves, which she wanted to save until she had a full day to savour it—exploring the town of Beaulieu itself and then perhaps a drive through some of the surrounding countryside where she could park and explore.

If she set off early enough, she could probably complete her shopping chores this morning, which would leave her the whole afternoon free to explore. She closed her eyes blissfully, imagining herself in some secluded spot enjoying a lunch of fresh, crusty bread, home-made pâté and perhaps some of the local cheese, while from her vantage point she watched the river.

'Dreaming about your lover?'

Angrily, Livvy opened her eyes as Richard Field's harsh voice destroyed her pastoral fantasy.

The cat, sensing her tension, jumped down off her knee, dislodging the guidebook as she did so.

Livvy bent to retrieve it, but Richard Field beat her to it. He frowned as he handed it back to her.

'"The natural beauty and historical sights of the Dordogne",' he read, scanning the cover, his mouth curling into an open sneer as he remarked contemptuously, 'Hardly your style, I would have thought.'

Too angry to hide what she was feeling, Livvy snatched the book back off him, ignoring the sharp electric tingle that raced up her arm as her fingertips inadvertently touched the hard warmth of his hand.

'That's an arrogant and totally illogical statement,' she told him cuttingly. 'Despite what you seem to think, you *don't* know me or my tastes and personality. I'd be very suspicious of anyone's judgement if they claimed to know everything there was to know about another human being merely on the strength of twenty-four hours' very casual acquaintance, but then of course I'm neglecting to take into account the insight into the female psyche which you seem to feel you have... an insight which, as far as I can ascertain, is based almost solely on prejudice...'

Livvy could see that she had surprised him.

'Are you trying to tell me that *you* are genuinely more interested in exploring the history of the area than...?'

'I'm not trying to tell you anything,' Livvy assured him, adding pointedly, 'I wouldn't waste my breath.'

'I should have thought a man-made cavern of expensive, exclusive shops where you could spend someone else's money would be of more interest to you than somewhere like this,' he told her, gesturing towards the open page of the guide and its description of caves.

'If that were the case, I wouldn't be here, would I?' Livvy told him sweetly.

As she walked past him and into the kitchen, she was surprised to discover that, along with a sweet sense of triumph, she also felt oddly sorry for him. He was obviously a wealthy man; had his cynical attitude towards her sex been the result of a relationship with the kind of woman he now accused her of being?

If so, she confessed to being a little surprised. She would have thought him too aware, too distrustful, too armoured by his own hardness to be vulnerable to that kind of woman; to any kind of woman, in fact, since he seemed so plainly to dislike and distrust her sex.

It pleased her, though, that she had managed to silence him; and to stand up to him.

Her sense of self-respect slightly restored, she went upstairs to collect her jacket and Gale's list. *Slightly* restored, but truthfully it would take more than merely walking away from a verbal exchange with him, having the last word, to wipe out the memory of that kiss he had forced on her.

She paused uncomfortably at the top of the stairs, forced to acknowledge that it wasn't so much the memory of his kiss which jarred, but her own unexpected reaction to it.

When she came back downstairs there was no sign of him, although she could see a fishing-rod and some fishing tackle on the ground next to the BMW.

As she climbed into her own car, she stifled a small pang of envy. As a child she had thoroughly enjoyed the hours she had spent watching her grandfather fish, and later, while she was still young enough not to be aware that fishing wasn't something that girls did, to listen eagerly and learn from him while he explained its skills.

Beaulieu was everything the guidebooks had promised it would be and more, but Livvy firmly refused to give in to the temptation to start exploring its ancient streets straight away, reminding herself that work must come first, pleasure afterwards.

Even so, she could not resist the temptation of wandering through the market, pausing to enjoy the wonderful aromas from the stalls, admiring the contrast between the sharp, rich colours of the vegetables and fruit on one stall, and the softer, pale colours of the massed bunches of flowers on another.

On impulse, she stopped and bought herself a bunch. They would brighten up the dullness of the farmhouse kitchen, and she thought she had seen a large earthenware jug she could put them in.

Tempting though it was to linger, she forced herself to move on, pausing briefly to check the address of the plumbers' merchant from the list Gale had given her.

Unexpectedly, when she eventually found it, it was tucked away down a pretty, narrow side-street of ancient houses that looked almost as though they had been untouched since they had first been built, the frothing brilliance of bright scarlet geraniums planted in window

boxes outside the upper windows breaking up the
weathered softness of the stone.

The contrast between the age of the building and the
modern display of goods inside it took her slightly aback
at first.

The man who came to assist her displayed all the
charm and flirtatiousness for which the French male was
so famous, or so notorious, depending upon which side
of the sexual fence one looked at it from.

His eyes lit up appreciatively as he studied Livvy with
discreet male competence. It said a lot for his *savoir-
faire* that he didn't drop his slightly flirtatious and
flattering manner towards her once she outlined the
business which had brought her to him, Livvy reflected
to herself with amused appreciation.

'Yes, I believe I recall *madame* your cousin,' he agreed
with commendable tact. 'You say she has supplied you
with a list of her requirements...'

'Yes, but before I give you the order, she wishes me
to secure a definite delivery date,' Livvy told him firmly.

It took them almost an hour to reach an agreement.
Provided his suppliers had the goods in stock, he could
definitely promise to start work at the beginning of
September, he assured her.

Gravely, Livvy told him that she would convey that
information to her cousin.

As she stepped outside into the street, he followed her,
removing from her the burden of her flowers while she
put the brochures and price lists he had given her safely
away with Gale's list.

As she turned to thank him and take her flowers, he
surprised her by lifting her hand to his lips and kissing
her fingertips with a theatrical flourish. Trying hard not

to giggle, Livvy retrieved her hand and started to turn away from him.

As she did so, she suddenly froze with shock at the unexpected sight of Richard Field, watching her with cold-eyed contempt less than a couple of yards away.

To her annoyance, Livvy knew she had started to flush. The owner of the plumbers' merchants had disappeared and she was alone in the narrow street with Richard Field.

'So much for this morning's protests,' he told her as he drew level with her. 'It seems my initial judgement of you was accurate after all.'

Livvy gritted her teeth. Of course, after having seen her at the *auberge* that first night, he would jump to that conclusion. He really had the most fervid and judgemental nature she had ever come across if he could genuinely misinterpret the totally innocent exchange he had just witnessed as some kind of passionate sexual liaison.

'If you must know, I hardly know the man,' Livvy told him crossly. 'He...'

She wasn't given any opportunity to continue or explain.

'Since when did knowing your partner matter to a woman like you? It's the conquest that excites your type, the thrill and danger of the risks you take.'

As she listened to him and compared her cautious and conventional personality to the picture he was drawing, Livvy was almost tempted to laugh, but the anger she could see in his face stopped her.

She could almost feel the tension emanating from him, reaching out to engulf her in its dangerous grip.

Instinctively she stepped back from him, tiny thrills of nervous alarm feathering along her sensitive skin.

For some reason her action seemed to increase his anger.

'It's a bit too late for the coy virgin act,' he told her contemptuously. 'It's obvious that it's a role for which you'd be seriously and laughably miscast.'

'That's the only way you can see women, isn't it?' Livvy retorted suddenly, as angry with him as he was with her. 'We're either sexual adventuresses or virgins, bad or good...' Her eyes flashed, her mouth curling with disdain as she gave full rein to her emotions.

'I feel really sorry for you. It must be hard work clinging on to such antediluvian views. You're the kind of man who if he marries will insist on his wife's being timid and totally inexperienced because you can't stand the thought of her comparing you to anyone else. You'll be terrified of her growing up and maturing into a real woman because if she does she'll discover that she hasn't married a real man. Why am I saying I feel sorry for *you*? *She's* the one I really feel sorry for.'

Livvy's eyes flashed again as her indignation and anger grew.

'You know nothing about me or my marriage...'

It wasn't just the raw fury in his voice that silenced her, Livvy acknowledged, as a peculiar leaden feeling developed in the pit of her stomach and her mouth suddenly went very dry.

'You're married...'

Her voice sounded squeaky and slightly shocked.

'I was,' he told her harshly, 'I'm not now.'

It must be the heat and the fact that she wasn't used to giving way so freely to her emotions that was making her feel so light-headed, Livvy reflected. Giving way to them . . . She wasn't even used to experiencing them . . .

She felt very shaky and sick all of a sudden. All the fight seemed to have gone out of her and she felt as though she wanted to crawl away somewhere quiet and safe.

'I . . . I must go. I've got some shopping to do . . .' Why did her voice sound so weak and hesitant, so emotional almost?

When he made no attempt to stop her, Livvy hurried past him, aware that he was walking in the opposite direction and into the building next to the plumbers' merchants which advertised office, secretarial and fax services.

Her heart thumping heavily, Livvy paused and turned round, frowning, as she stared at the building. Why had he gone in there? To contact George, perhaps, and alert him to what was happening?

If he knew where George was, he would be acting more in his interests if he persuaded him to get in touch with Gale so that they could sort out their differences, rather than adding further fuel to the dispute between them.

But then a man with his attitude towards women, towards marriage, was hardly likely to advocate reconciliation.

Her altercation with Richard Field, combined with the length of time she had spent in the plumbers' merchants, had taken up more time than Livvy had anticipated.

By the time she had completed her shopping, it was midday and too hot to countenance driving around in her car.

She could of course return to the farmhouse, but she didn't want to do that—not yet; and alternatively she could have a cup of coffee in one of the tempting cafés she had seen in the town and then spend a couple of hours exploring its shady medieval streets.

But if she did so, would she run the risk of bumping into Richard Field again?

Why should she let the thought of seeing him dictate to her what she could and could not do? If he wanted to think the worst of her, to condemn her and the whole female sex just because his own marriage hadn't worked out, then that was his problem, not hers.

It was not surprising that his marriage hadn't worked out, she decided, after storing her purchases in her car and retracing her steps to one of the cafés she had seen earlier.

What had she been like, Richard Field's wife? Livvy wondered as she sipped her coffee. Had she been the naïve, unawakened bride she had accused him of wanting earlier, or had it been a very different kind of woman who had brought him to view her sex with contempt and bitterness?

She put down her coffee-cup, frowning slightly. What did it matter what kind of woman she had been? It was of no interest to her.

Except that... Except that the man who had kissed her so angrily and punishingly yesterday, and who throughout their short acquaintance had treated her with aggression and contempt, had also unexpectedly, inexplicably and totally unwantedly physically aroused her so that, just for a heartbeat of time, while he held her, it had been as though he had been as shocked and confused by the passion which had exploded between them as she had been herself.

All nonsense, of course. She doubted that Richard Field would ever allow himself to admit that anything could shock or confuse him, and most especially not a woman.

She ordered another cup of coffee and drank it slowly, savouring its rich flavour, content simply to sit and enjoy her surroundings. A tiny smile twitched the corners of her mouth as she remembered the theatrical gallantry she had been treated to earlier. The French tradesman's equivalent of a British building site worker's wolf-whistle? Richard Field obviously hadn't seen it in that light.

Richard Field—there she went again, thinking about him.

Drat the man, she had come to Beaulieu to get away from him, not to waste time thinking about him.

It was mid-afternoon when Livvy eventually arrived back at the farmhouse. The BMW was parked in the yard but there was no sign of its owner anywhere, she discovered with relief.

She found the jug she had recalled seeing standing next to the dresser.

She had noticed a pretty French Provençal-style dinner service in one of the shop windows in Beaulieu, the central motif of the design a variety of farmyard an-imals, the border a soft mingling of pink and yellow checks. It would look good on the dresser's empty shelves.

She smiled ruefully to herself, half deriding her feminine home-making instincts.

One day she hoped she would marry and have a family, but for now she was perfectly content as she was, enjoying her independence and her career.

As she stored her purchases away in the fridge, she frowned, noticing that Richard Field had bought exactly the same local cheese as she had chosen for herself. Wryly she acknowledged that he would be even less pleased to discover that they shared a taste in common than she was herself.

It wasn't as hot as it had been, and the view of the river from her bedroom window tempted her to explore. She set off through the farmyard, following a footpath which seemed to go in the general direction of the river, obscured from view now by the trees.

The path led quite steeply downwards through the trees and when Livvy first broke through their cover and saw the river she couldn't help giving a small gasp of pleasure.

It was wider and deeper than she had expected and beautifully clear, so clear that she could see the speckled skins of the trout beneath the surface. Watching them, she was instantly reminded of sitting on a very similar riverbank with her grandfather, solemnly watching him cast his line, listening as he explained to her the skills required to lure his prey.

Smiling to herself, she walked upriver, pausing every now and again to study and admire her surroundings.

It was so peaceful here. Too peaceful for two almost teenage children? She frowned to herself, and then shook the thought off. Gale knew her children and their tastes far better than she did—and yet somehow or other she could not shake off the awareness that city-bred, sophisticated youngsters might not find the same pleasure in wading thigh-deep in crystal-clear water, tickling trout as she had once done.

As she had *once* done?

A wide grin curved her mouth as she looked at the river. Impulsively, before she could change her mind, she quickly stripped off her trainers and jeans, firmly knotting the ends of the cotton shirt she was wearing above her midriff. The water was probably deeper than it looked.

As she stepped down into it, she suppressed the gasp of shock that rose in her throat. She had forgotten how cold river water could be, but as she gritted her teeth and carefully waded deeper into the river the icy cold became a warm glow.

There was nothing, nothing quite like the pleasure and attraction of running water, she decided, nor the feel of water-smoothed stones beneath one's feet. It took her back almost instinctively to her childhood, to all the happy hours spent gathering very similar stones and using them to construct a series of complicated dams.

She and her cousins had whiled away many happy hours in such pursuits, vying with one another as to who could build the strongest dam.

Still smiling to herself, Livvy waded into the middle of the river and then stopped, surveying the water.

Ah, there was a likely spot. A nice, still, natural basin with a couple of good-sized rocks overhanging it. With any luck...

Carefully she waded back to the bank. She had been right about the depth of the water. It had been well over halfway up her thighs. Luckily, her briefs were still dry.

Leaving her clothes where she had removed them, she walked silently upstream until she reached the over-hanging rocks she had seen from the middle of the river.

Once there, she lay down carefully on them, making sure she was safely balanced before leaning over and peering down into the water.

Yes, she had been right... She could see the trout quite clearly, basking lazily in a sunlit patch of water half under the protection of the rocks.

Holding her breath, she leaned over very, very care-fully. The trick was to get her hand into the water without disturbing the fish.

Slowly now...

'What the hell do you think you're doing?'

Startled, Livvy tried to turn round and then realised that she was too precariously balanced and that she was going to fall into the river, but before she did her body was grabbed from behind, two strong male hands gripping her waist as Richard Field hauled her back and lifted her on to her feet.

'What do you think you're doing? Let go of me,' she demanded crossly as he swung her round to face him.

'What do I think *I'm* doing?'

He suddenly seemed to become aware of her semi-naked state, his eyes narrowing as his gaze skimmed her body, his hands tightening momentarily on her waist so that a sharp *frisson* of sensation raced over her skin. She could feel the rough maleness of the pads of his fingers. It was an almost caressive abrasiveness, an awareness of the contrast between the softness of her female flesh and the hardness of his maleness. Disturbed by her awareness of him, Livvy pulled against his imprisonment of her, her face flushing with self-consciousness.

No wonder he was looking at her like that. She must look a sight, clad in a pair of white briefs, with her shirt knotted up round her middle.

'Haven't you any more sense than to come creeping up on someone like that?' she demanded. 'I could have fallen in...'

'By the look of you, you already have,' he retorted crisply, and before Livvy could stop him he lifted one hand from her waist and ran it experimentally down her still damp side. The touch of his fingers, of his palm against the curve of her buttock and then the sensitive skin of her thigh, no matter how non-sexual it was intended to be, brought an outraged protest to her lips, and a rash of equally shocked goose-flesh to her skin; the shiver that ran up her spine lifted the tiny blonde hairs upwards in stiff, outraged reaction.

For a moment she was acutely aware of the contrast between them: of him, his body male and hard, clad in a dark cotton shirt, the sleeves rolled back to reveal brown, sinewy forearms, his jeans equally dark, an alien male figure bathed in black and gold against the sun, while in contrast she stood half-naked before him, her skin soft and pale, vulnerable to his view, and to his touch.

He seemed to sense something of what she was feeling because immediately he released her, frowning as he asked her, 'What were you doing...?'

'Tickling trout,' she told him, her chin lifting as she saw first the surprise and then the amusement lightening his expression.

'What? I don't suppose it occurred to you that it might be easier to use a rod and line?' He was openly mocking her now.

'If I had one, I suppose I might, although I was taught that it requires far more skill to land the fish with one's bare hands than to bait a hook and simply wait for it to impale itself...'

She saw his eyebrows rise.

'I think there's a large lobby of fishermen who would take umbrage with you at such a denigration of their skills,' he told her drily.

He was still watching her, but there was curiosity in his gaze now, curiosity and interest.

'You like fishing?' he asked her, almost as though he was expecting her to deny it.

'Yes,' she told him, and then admitted honestly, 'but only if I can put the fish back alive. My grandfather used to get very cross with me for refusing to eat what we caught. And even now I'm still not overfond of trout.'

'Your grandfather?'

'Mmm... He taught me...all of us...he and my grandmother.' She paused, frowning. Why was she telling him this? He couldn't really be interested. She turned away from him, but her still damp foot slipped on a piece of moss. As she felt herself start to fall backwards, she cried out. Instantly, Richard reached for her, dragging her back from the edge of the overhang, swinging her away from it and into his arms.

Immediately, she froze.

It was the worst, the most betraying thing she could have done, she acknowledged a heartbeat of time later, as she looked up into his face and saw the expression in his eyes.

Impossible for him not to be aware of the reason for that brief shudder which had ripped through her body, for him *not* to have recognised the sexual orientation, for him not to be able to see as clearly as she could *feel* that beneath her thin shirt her nipples were hard with arousal and that the reason her heart was beating so fast had nothing at all to do with the shock of almost falling into the river and everything to do with the fact that she was standing so close to him.

She watched motionless, her eyes blind with shocked self-knowledge as he slowly lowered his head. Her tongue-tip touched her lips. She gave a small, aching sigh.

'Olivia...'

She heard him say her name, felt the warmth of his breath whispering against her lips, her body quivered, and then somewhere behind them in the trees a bird made a noisy shriek of protest.

Immediately the realisation of what she was doing, of what she was *inviting* jolted through her, and Livvy pulled back from him, her face on fire with shock and guilt.

It came as no surprise that he let her go immediately. What on earth had come over her? she asked herself as she hurried away from him to where she had left her jeans and trainers. Thank goodness that bird had disturbed them when it had... Otherwise...

Otherwise... She gave a small shudder, fiercely clamping down on the images her mind was taunting her with.

CHAPTER SEVEN

WHAT on earth was happening to her? Livvy fumed helplessly as she rubbed her damp hair dry and then reached for her hairdryer; her face flamed as she recalled the scene by the river's edge. Why, oh, why had she given in to that ridiculously childish impulse to strip off and resurrect that old childhood pleasure?

No wonder Richard had looked at her the way he had. He must have thought she had taken leave of her senses. Either that, or... Her flush deepened, a dazed, helpless look darkening her eyes and softening her expression. Her lips parted slightly as her heart missed a small beat and then she caught sight of herself in the mirror and instantly banished that dangerous, weakening feeling.

Later, dressed, her hair plaited, thankful to discover that she had the kitchen to herself, she took herself severely to task.

It simply would not do, this idiotic foolishness... this dangerous and reprehensible awareness of Richard Field as a man... a very male man... a man to whom, for some unfathomable reason, she was dangerously attracted.

Attracted to Richard Field... her? Impossible. Surely she was far too sensible, had her feet planted far too firmly and safely on the ground to allow her emotions or her body to be swayed by a man who her brain told her had none of the qualities she really admired.

Look at his attitude towards women for a start. She frowned as she placed a large pile of books she had brought downstairs with her on the kitchen table. She had come here to the Dordogne to work as well as relax. Whether or not she decided to take up the school's offer of promotion, she still had next term's work to prepare.

The head had demurred at first when she had suggested French conversation classes, but Livvy's enthusiasm had brought him round and he had been generous in his praise at the end of the school year when it had been obvious that the conversation classes had had a beneficial effect on her pupil's grammatical grasp of the French language.

Next term, Livvy had planned to take her more advanced pupils a step further forward, initially planning to set them modern French novels to read, but after consideration changing her plans and substituting instead French film videos.

It was no use expecting a class of modern fourteen-year-olds to wax enthusiastic over the French classics, she acknowledged, no matter how much she would have enjoyed re-reading them, which was why she had bought herself a selection of the more popular French paperbacks to read over the holidays.

Right now, though, what she wanted to do was to sit down and do some work on the things she wanted to cover during the next term, the first of the new school year.

And thinking about Richard Field and the way he had held her, the way she had felt when he touched her, the way she had looked at him and for one dizzying, breathless second had actually wanted, yearned and ached for the feel of his mouth on hers, was not going to be conducive to such work.

It took her over half an hour to successfully, if not exactly banish Richard from her thoughts, then at least manage to restrict him to a relatively distant part of her mind.

She stopped once to make herself some coffee and to eat some of the crusty fresh bread she had bought, wondering as she did so where Richard had gone to.

He must have left while she was upstairs getting changed and, contradictorily, instead of being pleased that she had the farmhouse to herself, she realised that she was actually missing his presence, wondering where he was...what he was doing...who he was with.

No doubt when he did come back and found that she had taken possession of the kitchen table, and with it the kitchen itself, he probably wouldn't be too pleased, she reflected as she looked a little guiltily at the mass of books and papers she had spread over the table.

After all, where else could she work? The dim, dark sitting-room-cum-parlour had no table or desk in it, the other downstairs rooms were virtually unfurnished, and besides, she felt more comfortable in the kitchen, with the comforting warmth and noise of the range and the cat, who had come inside with her, curled up asleep on the floor in front of it. For a farmyard creature, it was proving surprisingly adaptable to domesticity. Unlike a certain male. She nibbled the end of her pen thoughtfully. Why was he so antagonistic towards her sex?

She suspected that the curt, 'I was. I'm not now,' response he had made to her involuntary shocked, 'You're married?' probably held the answers, or some of them.

What had his wife been like? she wondered. He must have loved her intensely for her to have hurt him so badly. How long had she...had they...?

'Never get involved with a divorced man,' Jenny had once told her with world-weary cynicism after the break-up of yet another romance. 'They're either so hung up on their ex-wives that they just can't see anyone else, or they're so bitter and resentful that they take it out on you. Either way, they're trouble.'

Livvy's frown deepened. She had laughed then, thinking that her friend was guilty of exaggeration. But people *were* affected by what they experienced in life, scarred sometimes...

She caught herself up quickly. How or why Richard Field had acquired his cynical and totally wrong-headed view of the female sex was nothing to do with her, and if she was wise she would make sure it stayed that way.

It should be easy enough after all. There was certainly nothing he had said or done that could have caused this anxiety she was feeling, this uncertainty whether she was capable of maintaining a sensible emotional distance between them. Nothing whatsoever.

Just because physically he had aroused her...just because this afternoon, when he had looked at her, touched her...

She tensed as she heard the BMW drive into the yard, caution and common sense urging her to collect her things together and leave before he came in. What after all was the point in risking another confrontation, or in reminding him of that brief heartbeat of time earlier when she had looked at him, looked at his mouth, her body and her eyes telling him nakedly and wantonly that she *wanted* him to kiss her?

Why should she go? She had nothing to be ashamed of. It had been a momentary lapse, that was all, but as she heard the door open she quickly bent her head over her work, raising it again only when she heard the noise he was making as he trundled the heavy replacement gas cylinder across the floor and towards the fridge.

For some reason she herself could not entirely understand, Livvy told him haughtily, 'There was no need for you to do that. Gale has an arrangement with Mr Dubois to have the gas replaced when necessary...'

'Fine, only what it seems *he* neglected to tell you or her is that he makes a surcharge on the canisters, and a connection fee. It seems to be a subject of great amusement at the garage where I got this stuff that he manages to make so much extra income out of gullible visitors by charging them almost double what the gas costs him and then making a profit on top of that reconnecting the thing for them. Amusement and envy. The garage owner told me he's tired of supplying him with rusty connections which, it seems, only Monsieur Dubois has a wrench suitable for unfastening.'

'It's only natural that he should want to make a profit on us,' Livvy told him lamely.

'A profit, yes—a laughing-stock is something else.'

There was nothing Livvy could say.

But it seemed that Richard Field had not finished.

'Of course, for all I know, you might have come to some *special* arrangement with him... The payment of a small *douceur* in exchange for his prompt service, perhaps...'

Livvy flushed as she read the real meaning behind his sneered words. She was almost shaking as she stood up and told him furiously, 'You have no right to imply any such thing. I would *never...*' She broke off, reminding herself that she had no need to defend herself to him, nor surely any reason to feel not just weak and shaky with the force of her anger, but frighteningly close to tears as well.

'Besides,' she challenged him, fighting to suppress her weakness, 'according to you, Monsieur Dubois believes that I'm *your* mistress.'

'All the more reason for him to take pleasure in having you,' he told her brutally.

It was more than Livvy could stand. Trembling from head to foot, her face white with anguish, she swept her hand outwards in a fierce movement of rejection, accidentally dislodging some of her papers from the table as she did so.

'*Having* me?' Her mouth trembled. 'Is that how you think of a sexual relationship between a man and a woman? If so, I'm not surprised that——'

Abruptly, she stopped herself, appalled by what she was doing, by what she had been about to say. Let him demean himself if he wished to do so; there was no need for her to stoop down to his level.

'So how do *you* think of a sexual relationship between a man and a woman...?'

The unexpected question caught her off guard. He was standing next to the fridge, his face half in shadow so that she couldn't read his expression. His voice was deceptively soft.

A tiny, fierce shiver ran over her skin. She couldn't help herself. As she closed her eyes, she had a momentary mental image of the two of them together, his body lean, hard, male, arched protectively over hers, smaller, paler, softly feminine and vulnerable, but willingly, achingly open to him.

She bit down hard on her bottom lip, appalled by the intensity and clarity of her vision.

'Well?'

His voice was still soft, but very, very determined. She gave another shiver, releasing her lip, feeling its swollen pressure where she had bitten it.

'I think of it as an equal and mutual sharing of themselves with one another, a partnership in which the two people concerned complement one another and make one another whole; in which there is no taking, no selfish greed, no desire to hurt or dominate the other person. I think of it as a very special and privileged human experience which far too many people denigrate and destroy.'

Her voice was shaking, Livvy recognised as she turned away from him. What had come over her? She had not meant to tell him any of that; even if it was the truth. She felt sick at the thought of how much of herself she had revealed to him. She tensed, waiting for his jeering laughter, his caustic mockery and contempt, but instead of the harshness she had expected his voice sounded faintly rough, almost as though his throat was slightly sore as he told her, 'Only an idealistic fool thinks things like that.'

Still shaking slightly, Livvy bent down to pick up her papers, not realising until she did so that he had moved and that he too was bending to retrieve them.

She saw him frowning as he studied them. 'You're a teacher?'

She could hear the disbelief in his voice and in other circumstances she might almost have been amused.

Instead she responded quietly, 'Yes. Why? Have you got a thing against them as well as women? Don't tell me,' she added bitterly. 'Let me guess. Your first teacher was a woman and you felt rejected when she didn't devote all her attention to you...'

'Yes. My first teacher was a woman,' he agreed gravely. 'Isn't every man's? And, yes, I suppose she did reject me in a sense. She *left* my father when I was two years old to go and live with her lover. She didn't want to leave me behind, or so she told me years later. She simply didn't have any choice. Her lover didn't like children and certainly didn't want to be burdened with another man's. She felt I'd be better off with my father...'

If he had heard her shocked gasp of pity, he wasn't making any response to it, Livvy realised thankfully, as she cursed her runaway tongue for its unwitting cruelty. She had never meant to hurt him nor to pry; she had simply lashed out in retaliation against the pain he had caused her.

'My father did the best he could, but he had a business to run, a life to live, and at least at the boarding-school he sent me to I had the company of other children.'

'Boarding-school?'

He gave her a wry look. 'Why so shocked? It was a very good school. What do you teach?' he asked her, changing the subject.

'French,' Livvy told him shakily.

He had picked up one of the paperbacks she had bought and was studying it.

'It's for my French conversation classes. The girls, are at an age where it's pointless trying to interest them in the classics. I've managed to persuade the head to allow me to show French videos. There'll be a question and answer session afterwards, and a discussion group, so that they'll have to concentrate on what they're watching.'

'Is it a single-sex school?' he asked her, as he studied the paperback he was holding.

'No,' Livvy responded, adding wryly, 'I know it isn't going to be easy finding something equally appealing to the boys as well as the girls, but . . .'

'Computer games . . .' he told her.

Livvy stared at him, watching as his frown disappeared and a small smile tugged at the corners of his mouth.

'I'm sorry. I'm interfering, aren't I? It's just that both my stepbrothers who are in their teens are mad on computer games . . .'

'Your father remarried, then?' Suddenly, for no reason she could think of, Livvy found that her heart was lifting, her own mouth starting to curve into a responsive smile.

'Eventually.'

'And you . . . you don't mind . . . ?'

'No. My stepmother has made him very happy. She was his secretary for many years and knew him very well.'

'And you get on well with her . . . ?'

Livvy wasn't sure why it suddenly seemed important to ask that question, why it should matter to her that there might be one woman whom he could like and respect.

When he hesitated, she found that she was holding her breath, willing him not to retreat from her, willing him to answer her. 'I do now,' he said eventually.

'Now?'

His smile had gone. 'She didn't want me to get married. She didn't care for my wife. Perhaps if I'd listened to her...' He stopped abruptly and Livvy flushed, realising how inquisitive she was being. Would he put it down to mere feminine nosiness and curiosity, or would he guess that her interest had a much more personal motivation? What personal motivation? she asked herself nervously. Hadn't she already agreed with herself that she was not going to allow herself to develop any personal interest in him? That it was far too dangerous to do so?

'I get on very well with her,' he told her, but his tone had become slightly brusque. Sensitively, Livvy recognised it and stopped herself from asking any more questions.

Instead she said as lightly as she could, 'Computer games... Thanks for the tip. I suspect you're probably right. I would never have thought of it myself. They aren't something that appeals to me...my brain just doesn't work in that kind of way.'

She looked up and caught the fleeting look of surprise in his eyes.

'It's very honest of you to admit it.'

It was Livvy's turn to look surprised. 'We all have our vulnerabilities and weaknesses,' she told him. 'I've never seen any point in trying to deny mine. I have a gift for languages which in its way involves a form of logic, but it isn't the same kind of logic needed to work out mathematical sequences or become computer-adept, and besides...'

'It's not very feminine. Like knowing how to change a tyre. Very flattering to the male ego.'

His voice had hardened again and Livvy gritted her teeth. Why on earth was it that, every time they seemed to be talking to one another as normal human beings, he had to spoil everything by reverting to challenging her ... accusing her ...

Perhaps because it was his only way of protecting and defending himself. From her? Why should he need to? She didn't pose any threat to him, did she?

He placed her papers on the table and turned away from her, walking over to the fridge.

Livvy tried to recapture her interest in her work, to concentrate on what she was supposed to be doing, but somehow her attention kept drifting away from the papers in front of her and in the direction of the man working quietly and determinedly in the corner of the room. He had his back to her and she could see the muscles moving in his back as he applied the wrench to the rusty connections of the existing gas container. He was wearing a shirt, but the pressure needed to loosen the connections was pulling it taut against his flesh.

A tiny feather-light sigh of sensation brushed against her skin, making her stomach muscles quiver and then tense.

She could feel her body getting hot, her mouth going dry. What would have happened this afternoon if she hadn't pulled away when she had?

She closed her eyes briefly, mentally imagining him without his shirt, his skin sleek and smooth, clinging supplely to his muscles.

She heard the small grunt of satisfaction he made as the first connection came free and her eyes opened.

This afternoon, standing close to him, she had caught the hot, musky scent of his sweat. And had been aroused by it? Just as she was now being aroused by her own thoughts. No! How ridiculous. Only infatuated teenagers or women in love reacted like that to such small stimuli.

Women in love!

She could feel the small hairs on the nape of her neck standing on end as the shock engulfed her in an ice-cold *frisson* of fear.

In love with Richard Field? Impossible ... How could she be?

Blindly she tried to focus on her work, to ignore his presence at the other end of the room.

Why on earth had George behaved so irrationally, allowing Richard Field to come down here, not telling Gale what he was doing? And how could she, even in her wildest imagination, allow herself to fall in love with a man who could behave as callously and uncaringly towards her sex as Richard Field did?

All right, so maybe this evening she *had* had a brief glimpse into his past, had sensed the pain he must have suffered when his mother left him and when his marriage broke up, but none of that altered the fact that he had been openly contemptuous and wrong about her.

Any woman falling in love with that kind of man was just asking to be hurt.

'There, that should do it.'

At any other time the male satisfaction in his voice would have made her smile; as it was, instead she tensed, refusing to look up from her work.

What was he doing, hovering over her? Why didn't he go away and leave her alone? He was standing behind her now, close enough for her to sense his presence, so much so that she could feel her body trembling in response to it.

'I ought to ring Gale... She'll want a full report on how I got on with the plumber...'

She was talking quickly, wildly almost, desperate to fill the dangerously intense silence between them, to defend herself against the miasma of awareness that threatened her. Would her cousin still want to go ahead with her plans if George was trying to sell the farmhouse?

'The plumber?' Richard Field was questioning her.

'Yes... I went to see him this morning. Gale wants——'

'Was that the plumber I saw you speaking with in Beaulieu?'

Livvy tensed. 'Yes, as a matter of fact it was,' she agreed.

Inadvertently she turned round, her stomach lurching. He was standing even closer to her than she had imagined. She could see the faint beginnings of the new beard growing along his jaw. There was a smudge of oil on his cheek; it made him look younger, more approachable, very human and in some odd way almost vulnerable. She had to stop herself from reaching up and smoothing it away.

The cat too was affected by his closeness. It uncurled itself and stood up, arching its back and then rubbed itself against his legs, purring loudly.

Almost absently, he bent down and picked it up, stroking it.

'*You* should be outside, not in here,' he told it. He was frowning again, Livvy recognised. Not at the cat, but at her.

'This is still Gale's home,' she told him defensively. 'She has every right——'

'As I understand it, it belongs to both Gale and George,' Richard Field interrupted her curtly. 'Does George know, I wonder, how Gale plans to spend his money? Or will she just present him with a *fait accompli* just as she always does? She treats him like an extra child, not a man. No wonder...'

The cat made a small squark of protest as he put it down.

'I need a shower,' he told her, then added curtly, 'I suppose it's too much to hope that I might be allowed just some small space on the table on which to eat my meal?'

'I'll be finished before you come back down,' Livvy assured him, equally curtly.

He was so changeable, so unfathomable, almost human one minute and then the next almost aggressively unpleasant and cold towards her.

She bent her head back over her work and didn't raise it again until she had heard the door close behind him. A shower, he had said.

She shivered beneath the thrill of wanton fire that ran through her as she pictured his naked body and then hastily denied the image and its potent effect on her.

'And as for you, you traitress,' she accused the cat, as it leapt on to her lap, 'you have absolutely no taste, do you know that? No sense of female solidarity; if you did, you'd have scratched him, not fawned all over him in that foolish, adoring manner.'

'I forgot my jacket.'

Livvy flushed beetroot-red as she realised that Richard was standing right behind her and that he must have overheard every word she had just said. She hadn't even heard him come back into the kitchen, and she certainly could not turn round now and give him the satisfaction of seeing her scarlet face.

It was enough that she had heard the amusement in his voice.

CHAPTER EIGHT

'AND you can see from the formation of them where over thousands of years the pressure of the water has worn away the softer rock to form these caves.'

'Have they ever been inhabited?' Livvy asked the guide curiously, as he paused to allow the tour to pause and acknowledge with awe the cavern that nature had created.

It was icy cold down here beneath the surface, especially after the heat of the summer sun outside, but Livvy had paid attention to the warnings in her guide-book and had dressed appropriately for her visit to the caves. Her question had been prompted by her awareness that, in other parts of France, along the Loire valley for instance and at other ancient sites, the caves there had been inhabited until quite recently.

Waiting now for the guide to answer her, she remembered too reading that in the pitifully war-torn country which had been Yugoslavia refugees were having to resort to making their homes in the same caves which their parents and grandparents had inhabited during the Second World War. Now, glancing around the icy coldness of the cavern, she tried to envisage how it would feel to have to make such a place one's home.

Several tunnels lay off the main gallery and she could well imagine the warren of passageways and caves which must honeycomb this subterranean world.

Like Theseus, though, in his quest to vanquish the Minotaur, one would need to be very sure of knowing one's way around such a very complicated maze.

Such places had always both fascinated and repelled her. She could still vividly remember her first visit to the caves at Inglewhite at home; the shock of the icy cold air; the awe at the size of the huge stalagmites and stalactites. Stalactites hung on tight to the ceiling, stalagmites grew upwards from the floor with all their might, the guide there had told her informatively.

She smiled ruefully to herself now while she listened to the guide responding to her question.

When she had taken her own class on a similar trip, they had scorned such homely explanations, although she had recognised that same look of awe and fascination in their eyes as even the 'coolest' members of 5V witnessed the effect of the relentless power of nature.

'That's nothing,' one of the boys had derided when they had entered the largest cavern, its ceiling so high above them that it was almost impossible to see it. 'A semtex bomb could make a hole twice this size in seconds... this took nature millions of years.'

'It takes man to detonate a bomb,' Livvy had told him. 'And man can always be stopped. Nature can't...'

It had been the lake which had impressed them all the most, though; so deep that no one had even truly plumbed its depths, and so cold that it was unsafe for even the strongest diver to stay below the surface for very long.

Their guide was directing them down a narrow passageway. Livvy had been lucky; there were only half a dozen other people on this afternoon tour. Their guide was a young geology student, a trifle earnest perhaps, but interesting none the less.

'I shouldn't like to be down here if there was a flood,' someone commented.

Livvy felt the brief *frisson* of fear that ran through the small group.

'We are safe enough here,' the guide assured them with a smile, 'but there are other parts...other passageways and caves.' He gave a brief shrug. 'We do not allow the public to endanger themselves in them, though.'

As he painstakingly explained the safety precautions they used, Livvy found her attention drifting slightly.

There had been no sign of Richard Field when she'd left this morning. Not that she minded, of course. The less they saw of one another, the better, as far as she was concerned.

It was just as well he possessed that blind prejudiced view of her and that he so patently disapproved of and disliked her, otherwise...

Otherwise what? Just because his kisses had made her feel...

They made her feel *nothing*, she told herself firmly. Nothing at all.

While their guide was explaining the geological make-up of the cave system, another tour group arrived in the cavern; schoolchildren, noisy and excited as they discovered the possibilities of the cavern's echo effect. They were younger than her own class. Livvy sympathised with the slightly tense-looking young woman who was obviously their teacher.

One of the boys, his face turned upwards to stare at the ceiling, backed accidentally into Livvy.

When the teacher hurried across to remonstrate with him and apologise, Livvy smiled at her. 'Don't worry about it,' she told her. 'I've been there myself...'

'You're a teacher?' the other girl queried.

She was about Livvy's own age, small and very French-looking, with her immaculate bobbed shiny dark hair, pristine shirt and jeans and soft Gucci loafers.

The same clothes worn by *her* would never have managed to look quite as chic as they did on this girl, Livvy reflected, and then acknowledged wryly to herself that a British schoolteacher's salary was hardly likely to stretch to what looked like a genuine pair of Gucci shoes.

'Yes, although my class is slightly older.'

They chatted for several seconds, but it wasn't until the other girl introduced herself and asked what subject Livvy specialised in that she realised that Livvy herself was not actually French.

Her astonishment when she discovered her nationality was rather flattering, Livvy acknowledged, although she was quick to explain that one of the reasons her French was so good was due to the holidays she had spent with her French relatives.

'*Oui*, that is the very best way to become fluent in another language,' the other girl agreed.

Her name was Marie-Louise Fernier and she had returned to teaching part-time following the birth of her son, she explained to Livvy as they chatted. When she learned that Livvy was staying locally, she immediately suggested that Livvy might like to look round the school.

'Perhaps we could have lunch together,' Marie-Louise added, 'I should enjoy that.'

'Lunch would be lovely,' Livvy agreed. It would also be interesting to get an informal look at close hand at a French school.

'Would tomorrow be too soon?' Marie-Louise asked her. 'Only, after tomorrow I do not work again until next week.'

'Tomorrow will be fine,' Livvy assured her. 'Where shall I meet you?'

'If you would like to come direct to the school,' Marie-Louise suggested. 'It is quite easy to find, a kilometre outside Beaulieu. If you could be there for twelve, we could have lunch and then in the afternoon I could show you over the school.'

After she had made a note of Marie-Louise's directions, Livvy realised that the rest of her tour had moved on. Excusing herself, she hurried to join them.

She would enjoy having lunch with the Frenchwoman, she acknowledged; it would be interesting to talk to her as a colleague and to compare the methods they used. Despite the fact that she had come to the Dordogne for solitude, she was already looking forward to seeing Marie-Louise again.

It would do her good to have something else to think about, something to take her mind off Richard Field and all the confusing and dangerous emotions he managed to arouse in her.

'You are here alone?' Marie-Louise had asked her, and she had been very quick to confirm that this was the case.

But it was the truth, after all. All right, so technically Richard Field was sharing the house with her, and the farmer seemed to have leapt to the conclusion because of that fact that they were together, a pair... lovers.

Lovers... A fine *frisson* of sensation, which had nothing to do with the fact that she had just emerged into the warm sunlight from the coldness of the caves, ran tauntingly over her skin.

'Had a good day?'

Livvy couldn't conceal her astonishment. She paused in the act of pouring herself a cup of coffee and turned to look at Richard Field.

He had walked into the kitchen a few minutes ago and, although she had pretended not to notice him, irritatingly, physically *and* mentally as well, she seemed to be extra-sensitive to his presence, her nerves on edge, her muscles tight and tense, and even her skin extraordinarily sensitive...so sensitive in fact that she could almost feel the eddies in the air made by his movements.

If he'd actually physically touched her, she couldn't have reacted more, she recognised edgily. It was ridiculous that he should have this effect on her, especially in view of what she knew about him and his opinions of her.

'Yes, fine. Have you?' she responded tersely without looking at him.

'Mmm...I went fishing...'

Livvy could feel her skin starting to burn. Fishing. It was hardly the most erotic of words and yet, as she heard him say it, a most extraordinary feeling of physically sensual awareness came over her.

For a moment she actually felt as she had done when they had stood together by the river, her heart pounding, her senses aware of everything about him, but most especially the fact that he was standing so close to her, holding her, touching her, his mouth only inches away from her own.

'Where have you been...?'

'I—er——' She felt dazed, giddy, foolishly, dangerously light-headed. Pull yourself together, she warned herself fiercely. Just because for once his voice had sounded soft, gentle, almost provocatively teasing, as though he too was remembering...

'I visited the caves,' she told him huskily.

'I thought tomorrow I might visit Cahors,' he told her, adding astoundingly, 'Perhaps you'd like to come with me. We could have lunch somewhere together, maybe...'

Livvy stared at him in shock. 'No...no, I'm sorry, I can't. I've already made arrangements... I'm having lunch with someone else...'

She was gabbling, she recognised shakily, but then she would defy anyone not to betray their feelings if they were in her shoes. The shock of hearing Richard actually suggest that they spend some time together, actually ask her to have lunch with him after the way he had behaved towards her, was enough to send anyone off balance.

As she looked into his face and saw the way it was closing, hardening, she had to suppress a wild urge to cry out in protest, to say that he had got it all wrong...that it was not that she didn't *want* to accept his invitation, to explain that it had come as such a shock.

'I see...'

His voice was cold and hard. As cold and hard as his face.

He was turning away from her, *walking* away from her. Livvy bit down hard on her lip to stop herself from calling him back. It was obvious what he was thinking, but what was the point in trying to explain? He obviously thought she had picked up some man and arranged to see him again.

Something dangerous and vulnerable inside her ached pitifully, but she refused to give in to it. After all, wasn't it really safer, wiser to let him think the worst of her? To ignore that ridiculous yearning to hear over and over again that gentle, almost tender, intonation to his voice which surely had to be a product of her ridiculously overcharged imagination?

And if it hadn't been... It had, she told herself firmly. After all, there was no way he could possibly feel any tenderness towards her.

'Good lunch, was it?'

Livvy tensed as she heard the sarcasm splintering through Richard Field's voice.

She had returned to the farmhouse less than half an hour ago, half expecting to find that Richard was still out, but instead she had discovered that he had returned before her.

'Yes, as a matter of fact it was,' she replied calmly. 'Very enjoyable.'

She warned herself that there was no point in deliberately goading him, and then asked herself ruefully what it was about him that drove her into over-reacting so irresponsibly.

She already knew how he believed she had spent her 'lunch'. Did she really look as though she had actually passed the afternoon indulging in some heavy sex-session, instead of enjoying a very pleasant lunch with another woman, accompanied by a very interesting discussion on different methods of teaching?

'And yours...?'

The look he gave her warned her that she had pushed him too far. 'Oh, for goodness' sake!' she exclaimed irately. 'Look, I *know* what you think, but you're totally wrong. *My* lunch date was another woman...a fellow teacher. I met her yesterday when I was touring the caves. She invited me to visit her school and to have lunch with her.'

When he made no response, she shrugged her shoulders and added impatiently, 'All right, don't believe me if you don't want to...I don't care.'

'Why didn't you tell me this yesterday?'

Livvy turned away from him uncomfortably. She knew quite well why she had led him on to believing the worst about her, and she knew equally well that there was no way she was going to answer his question honestly.

How could you tell a man like this one that your instincts, those perverse, feminine, rebellious and oh, so hard to control, deeply rooted, atavistic feelings which really had no place in the life of a sensible modern woman, had warned her that it would be dangerous to let him get too close to her...that it would be foolish to do or say anything which might bring down the barriers they had erected against one another, that it was safer to allow him to think the worst of her?

No, she couldn't tell him any of that. So instead, she shrugged again and, keeping her face turned away from him, said dismissively, 'Why should I?'

When he didn't make any response, she added edgily, 'It really didn't seem that important.'

'No? Then why tell me now?'

He was quick, she had to give him that, Livvy admitted, as she caught her breath. 'No reason,' she lied.

The look he was giving her made a mockery of her pretended insouciance.

'All right, I admit it. I *don't* like being judged—wrongly—as...as someone who's so sexually dependent that...' She was getting into deep water, she warned herself, and if she wasn't careful he was going to start asking her some very awkward questions, such as why it should matter to her what he thought of her or how he misjudged her. It didn't, of course, not one tiny little bit. It was just that...

'You mean you don't like the fact that I know exactly what you really are...'

'Oh, for heaven's sake, I've had enough of this. What you saw at the *auberge* wasn't what you thought at all... I *know* you won't accept this...I *know* you have some kind of...of problem which seems to make it impossible for you to view my sex other than with some ridiculously distorted bias, but that man you saw me with was *not* there with my consent, my desire, my agreement, or anything else. Far from it.

'He had followed me up from downstairs, using the fire exit. He caught hold of me before I could stop him, and what you seem determined to believe was a mutual desire for sex was in fact attempted rape. It was no thanks to you that he didn't succeed,' she added angrily. 'I really don't care *what* you think of me or even whether you believe me or not, but for the sake of the rest of my sex I would strongly counsel you to learn the distinguishing signs that say a woman is welcoming a man's advances or rejecting them.

'If I had wanted that...that oaf as my lover, do you honestly believe I'd have allowed him to maul me like that in the corridor, in public?' Her eyes flashed angrily, heightened colour burning her face. 'I suppose you're the kind of man who believes that no woman is ever raped against her will, that——'

'No...that's not true.'

The harshness of his denial shocked Livvy into silence, her anger suddenly spent, leaving her feeling oddly weak and close to tears.

She hadn't meant to say *anything* to him, to let him see how much his attitude towards her irked and distressed her, and now, in the silence filling the kitchen, she wished that she had remained silent.

He probably didn't believe her anyway, she reflected tiredly. He was probably far too used to holding on to the comfort of his antagonism to let go of it and admit that he had made a mistake.

She turned away from him, heading for the door.

'Why didn't you say something at the time?'

She stopped. Without turning round, she asked him huskily, 'Like what...please help me?' She looked at him over her shoulder and gave him a bitter smile.

She had just reached the door when she felt his hands on her arms. Her whole body tensed as he swung her round to face him. She could see the angry pulse beating in his jaw, smell the heat coming off his skin.

'You're enjoying doing this to me, aren't you?' he demanded through gritted teeth. 'You're loving every minute of it... You...'

He stopped as she made a tiny, choked sound of protest in her throat.

'My arms...you're hurting me,' Livvy protested fiercely, even though she knew it was more shock than pain that was making her tremble, and the fact was that the sensation of his skin against hers, of its warmth and strength, was producing tiny quivers of physical re-action inside her body which were a world away from what she was claiming to feel.

'I'm sorry.' He looked confused...bitter... anguished almost, she might have said, but then her gaze focused on his mouth, and the most extraordinary surge of emotion rose up inside her.

It took every ounce of will-power she possessed not to close her eyes and let her body sway softly into his, not to lift her head and offer him her mouth.

Quickly she pulled away from him, praying that he couldn't guess what she was feeling.

Perhaps he *was* right after all...perhaps secretly she was some kind of wanton... Perhaps *he* possessed some kind of magical power that totally transformed her per-sonality, made it impossible for her to resist him.

Yes, and it's called sexual chemistry, she told herself grimly, as he stepped back from her, setting her free to open the door and make her escape.

What on earth had possessed her to over-react like that? It was obvious that he hadn't believed a word she had said.

Which was perhaps just as well.

CHAPTER NINE

'So you still haven't been able to talk to George?' Livvy asked Gale anxiously.

As the kitchen door opened and Richard Field walked into the room, she pressed the receiver closer to her ear.

It was almost a week now since they had both arrived at the farmhouse, and she was growing increasingly anxious for the situation to be resolved. Not because Richard Field disturbed her personally; not because she found that she was disconcertingly aware of him as a man, and not even because of the unfamiliar feelings and emotions she was experiencing. No, it was none of those things; it was for Gale's sake that she wanted things sorted out, she assured herself firmly.

Even so, she found that she was turning round slightly, watching as Richard crossed over to the other side of the kitchen and proceeded to start making some coffee.

'George did telephone last night—from Japan,' she heard Gale telling her, 'but he rang off before I could tackle him about the farmhouse. I've a good mind to go and see Robert Forrest myself and ask him what he thinks he's playing at. George has a responsibility towards us as well as to his work.'

Livvy frowned as she caught the unfamiliar tremor in her cousin's voice. The situation was obviously placing far more of a strain on Gale than she had initially been prepared to admit.

'Livvy, I just don't know what to do,' Gale told her, confirming her suspicions. 'George has *never* behaved like this before. He's *always* put us first. I *know* his job's important... But he missed the boys' parents' day. He's never done that before... I went, of course, but I could tell how upset they both were by his absence. Roderick even asked me if... if George and I were going to get a divorce. I told him we weren't, but for all the time George is spending at home these days we might as well already be divorced.'

Beneath Gale's anger, Livvy could sense her bewilderment and pain. Her cousin needed her husband far more than she wanted to admit, Livvy recognised.

'He's still there, I suppose,' she asked Livvy, changing the subject. 'I hope you've made it clear to him that there's no way he can buy the farmhouse without my agreement. Really, the man must have the hide of a rhinoceros to persist in staying when...'

'He knows the situation, Gale,' Livvy cut her cousin off, all too conscious that Richard Field could probably hear what Gale was saying.

'Mmm... Well, I shall have a thing or two to say to George about what he's done when he does eventually come home. He should have discussed it with me first—giving the man a key and not saying a word to me about it... without giving any consideration at all to the situation he's placed you in.'

'George didn't know that I would be staying here, Gale,' Livvy felt bound to remind her cousin. 'I think I've managed to get everything sorted out with the plumber,' she added, wanting to get Gale off the subject of Richard Field. 'I've asked him to send the estimates direct to you. It sounds as though it's going to be rather

expensive,' she warned Gale. 'Perhaps in the circumstances you should wait...'

'As I'm having to wait for George to come home,'
Gale demanded crossly. 'No, thanks. I'll ring you just
as soon as I've spoken to him and found out what's going
on,' she added. 'I must go now. I'm taking Roderick to
his tennis lesson in half an hour.'

'That was Gale,' Livvy told Richard Field unnecessarily after she had replaced the receiver. There was no
need for her to explain her actions, nor to feel uncomfortable about them, and yet, idiotically, she did.

The smell of his freshly brewed coffee tantalised her
taste-buds; without discussing it or drawing up any
formal rules, they had somehow managed to evolve a
routine which brought them into as little contact with
one another as possible.

Richard Field spent most of his time away from the
farmhouse, exploring the region, Livvy assumed, but
today for some reason he had not gone out.

'How is she?'

The question caught her off guard. She stared at him
in surprise, searching his face for some sign of the irritation and dislike she had previously seen him exhibit
when he talked about her cousin but, a little to her surprise, she could find no evidence of it.

'She's f... She's very upset and worried,' she told him
quietly, pushing to one side the polite fib she had been
about to voice. 'I think she's just beginning to recognise
how much she needs George. The boys are missing him
too... I think she must be getting pretty desperate. She
was talking about getting in touch with George's boss
herself...'

She paused as she saw the quick frown he gave her.

'She's desperate to talk to George,' she told him defensively. 'Surely you can understand that? I *know* you don't have a very high opinion of the female sex, but Gale *is* George's wife and she has every right...'

She tensed with indignation as he turned away from her. He might at least have the courtesy to hear her out instead of turning his back on her and walking away, even if he didn't like what she was saying, but to her surprise, before she could protest at his rudeness, he had reached for a clean mug and was filling it with a second cup of coffee... When he turned back towards her, handing it to her, her jaw dropped slightly.

'Here,' he told her wryly. 'If we're going to have an in-depth argument on the subject of the rights that go with marriage in general, and your cousin's application of them in particular, then you might as well fortify yourself with this. If nothing else, it will give me an opportunity to have my say while you're drinking it.'

Livvy gaped at him. It almost sounded as though he actually enjoyed the thought of arguing with her... of *being* with her.

'There is nothing for us to argue about,' she told him loftily, as she tried to control the dizzy, heady feeling that was threatening what should have been far more rational thoughts. 'It's Gale's right as George's wife to expect him to discuss his plans with her. To share...'

'To share... It's easy to see that you've never been married nor involved in a long-term relationship. Ask anyone who has; they'll soon tell you that only foolish idealists believe that marriage is about sharing; the reality is that it's about power, power and control. Up until now, Gale has controlled George and their relationship, and now she's afraid that George might be escaping from her control she's starting to panic.'

'That's not true,' Livvy countered hotly. His cynicism appalled her. What must his own marriage have been like, for him to hold such views? Not a happy one, obviously. 'Gale loves and needs George. She might not always show it...it might not be obvious on the surface...she might have seemed to be the stronger one, the more powerful one,' she added as she caught the small sound of derision he made, 'but in reality...'

'In reality, what? She treats him like a child, orders him around and generally publicly humiliates him. Is that how she shows her need and love for him?'

'All right, she might sometimes seem to be slightly domineering,' Livvy admitted reluctantly, 'but that's only on the surface. Underneath...'

'You're obviously a hopeless romantic,' he told her roughly. 'You have to be if you think that.'

A hopeless romantic. Less than a week ago he had been accusing her of having a very different personality. As though he too was remembering that, he suddenly added abruptly, 'Mind you, you do have a vested interest in taking your cousin's side, don't you? You are both women.'

'I'm not taking her side,' Livvy told him. 'I'm just trying to point out that deep down she needs George.'

'Financially perhaps, but——'

'It isn't anything to do with money,' Livvy interrupted him angrily. 'It's emotionally that Gale needs George, although I don't suppose someone like you could ever understand that. You seem to be obsessed by money, determined to believe that it's the pivot of a relationship. Well, I for one would never put money before...'

'Before what?' he challenged her softly.

Livvy stared at him, suddenly aware of how dangerously off the subject she had travelled and on to ground which she was discovering was riddled with hidden potholes and quagmires.

Even so, she refused to be cowed by the hard, mocking look he was giving her. Lifting her chin, she told him firmly, 'Before my feelings.'

He laughed. 'So what *would* make you commit yourself exclusively to one man. Love?'

The cynicism in his eyes made her heart ache, but she was not going to back down, no matter how much he derided her.

'As a matter of fact, yes,' she told him bravely.

He stared at her for a long time before saying roughly, 'You're either a fool or a liar, and knowing what I do know about your sex . . .'

He didn't finish his sentence. He had no need to, Livvy reflected bitterly half an hour later as she drove her car down the farmhouse lane, still seething with the intensity of the emotions he had aroused in her.

What on earth had prompted her to expose herself to him like that? She had known before she opened her mouth what his reaction would be.

He might *seem* to have discarded his initial judgement of her as a promiscuous flirt, but she suspected that nothing could shift his entrenched and biased views of her sex.

As she turned out on to the main road, she admitted that she herself had been guilty of some bias. He had not liked it at all when she had met his final challenge by saying that, just because his own marriage had failed, it didn't mean that there was no such thing as a happy, successful marriage.

'What do you know about my marriage?' he had demanded aggressively.

'Nothing,' she had admitted, 'other than what you've told me. But it obviously didn't work. Your wife...'

'My wife left me for another man?' he interrupted her harshly. 'My wife only married me for one reason, and that reason was nothing to do with "love". She had the divorce settlement worked out before the ink on the licence was even dry.'

His bitterness had silenced Livvy, her eyes softening with a compassion she couldn't conceal. No matter how much she disagreed with his views and his attitude, it was impossible not to feel sympathy for the pain she could sense lying beneath his harsh words.

'You must have loved her.'

The soft words were said before she could recall them, and she knew at once that they were a mistake, an intrusion... a potential catalyst to the powerful emotions he was fighting to control.

'Loved her?' His eyes had glittered dark with disillusionment and pain. 'Loved her? No, but I thought I was *in* love, and she with me. I was wrong, though. What I had thought was "being in love" was in reality closer to lust—mere physical desire—but I was too young, and too idealistic, to recognise it at the time.'

The tone of his voice had made Livvy shiver. The words, 'Then why did you marry her?' stuck to her tongue like burrs to an animal's fur, but despite their irritation she refused to utter them, caution overwhelming curiosity.

'I know what you're thinking,' he told her. 'Go ahead, why don't you ask?'

Livvy had flushed at the scorn in his voice. 'It isn't any of my business,' she told him quietly, putting down her coffee-mug and preparing to turn away.

'No, you're damn right it isn't,' he had agreed, 'but I'll tell you anyway... Sexually she was the most...'

Livvy hadn't been able to stop herself; she had felt herself starting to flush, a deep burn of embarrassed and uncomfortable colour invading her body. It hurt hearing him talk like this, she had recognised. She had felt degraded somehow, not just by what he was saying, but by her own recognition of that sharp, plunging knife-turn stab of jealousy she had felt, that bitter awareness that she was not the kind of woman he could ever describe in those kind of terms, that her sexuality could ever have the power to entrap and hold a man against his will; and, along with her recognition of her pain and the reasons for it, had come bewilderment at her own reactions, at her even momentarily wanting to have that kind of sexual power, at wanting to be able to make him ache and burn with desire for her.

It had only lasted a second or so, a dangerous surge of primitive madness, soon banished to its rightful place.

She was not that kind of woman, nor did she really have any desire to be; and surely, if Richard Field had been foolish enough to get caught in that kind of trap, then he was not...

Not what? she asked herself shakily now. Not the kind of man who could appeal to her? Not the kind of man she could desire? Not the kind of man *she* could love?

*   *   *

She did her shopping, dawdling over it for as long as she could, stopping to have lunch in a café that overlooked a tree-lined square.

A small family were sitting at the next table to hers, the mother young and pretty, bloomingly pregnant, her two daughters, in the manner of Continental children, beautifully dressed and already touchingly and innocently aware of their femininity, allying themselves to their mother as they copied her actions, while at the same time enjoying flirting with their father while their mother looked on indulgently.

'I hope this one will be a boy,' Livvy heard her saying ruefully to her husband as she patted her stomach. 'I think I already have enough rivals.'

'A boy, another girl, I don't mind, just so long as you are well and happy,' her husband responded, leaning forward to touch her.

They looked so happy. It was a pity that Richard Field wasn't here with her to see them. With her? A small shiver shot through her. She was becoming dangerously obsessed with the man.

'What if you fall in love?' Jenny had teased her.

She had denied it, and in doing so had perhaps tempted fate?

But surely fate could not be cruel enough to allow her to fall in love with someone like Richard Field. And surely she had far too much sense?

She delayed going back to the farmhouse for as long as she could. Richard Field was on the telephone when she got back.

Tactfully, she didn't linger in the kitchen, placing her shopping on the table and then heading for the door without unpacking it. She could do that later when he had finished.

He had his back towards her and he was speaking quietly in monosyllables, as though he didn't want her to overhear what he was saying.

For some reason, that irked her. He had a right to want to keep his conversation private, of course, but there was no need for him to act as though she was the sort of person who was going to try deliberately to eavesdrop.

Because of the siting of the phone, she had to walk past him to get into the hall, but she kept as much distance between them as she could, intending to make it plain that she had no interest in either who he was talking to or what he was talking about, but naturally, since she had to walk within a foot or so of him, she couldn't help overhearing his low-voiced curt, 'No...I don't think that would be a good idea,' and could recognise that the person on the other end of the line was a man.

However, it wasn't until she was upstairs in her own room that she realised why his voice had been oddly familiar.

When she did, she put down her hairbrush and raced downstairs.

Richard was still in the kitchen but he had finished his call.

'That was George, wasn't it?' she demanded without preamble. 'On the phone just now, you were speaking with George?'

Her anxiety for Gale fuelled her sense of outrage.

'*Why* was he ringing you?' she asked him, something she would never normally have done. 'Did you tell him how upset Gale is . . . how worried . . . ?'

'Don't you think that's something Gale is perfectly capable of telling him herself?'

So it had been George. Livvy sat down, her voice quivering huskily with anger as she reminded him,

'How *can* she? He's in Japan and apparently so busy that he hasn't got time to speak to her properly. He had time to speak to you, though, didn't he?'

Disillusionment shadowed her voice. 'I suppose he wanted to know whether or not you've decided to buy this place,' she said dully, talking more to herself than to him. It shocked her that George, whom she had always thought of as so steady and reliable, was behaving like this, even though her conscience prompted her to acknowledge that Gale was perhaps not the easiest woman to live with, and that Richard had been right when he had told her that Gale was inclined to treat her husband more like another child than a man.

'Gale needs George,' she said unsteadily. 'And so do the boys. Can't you see what you're doing by encouraging him to behave like this? Just because *you've* got a grudge against the female sex, that's no reason for you to...to try to destroy Gale's marriage. You're not a man...you're a spoiled child. You——'

She didn't get any further. He was hauling her out of her seat, his hands locked round her arms, his body blocking her escape, even if she could have pulled away from him.

'So I'm not a man?'

It had been there between them all week, smouldering dangerously like a peat fire, just waiting for something to fan it into an open conflagration. And she had just supplied that something.

She tried to stop him, to make her protest, both verbally and physically, but deep down inside her there was some reckless, wanton part of her that actually gloried in what she had done, feeding on the shock of frightening excitement that ran through her.

When he kissed her, although neither of them acknowledged it, both of them knew that what was happening had nothing to do with the challenge she had given him and that it was simply an excuse, a sop to the convention demanded by their minds and their stubborn rejection of the deeper, far more primitive needs which really motivated them.

This time her mouth was aware of the taste and texture of his, aware of it and hungry for it, the hands she had curled into tight fists to push him away straightening, flattening against his chest, feeling its heat, moving exploratively over him, no longer pushing him away, exploration giving way to something that was far more of a caress. And all the time he was kissing her, holding her, his hands, like hers, spread flat against her skin, moving down over her back and on to her hips.

She tensed for a moment as he drew her closer to him, shivering as she recognised that the reason for her hesitation was not because she didn't want to experience the physical knowledge of his arousal, but because she did.

She trembled as she took that final self-betraying step, the small moan she made in her throat a surrender, not so much to him, but to her own feelings. He couldn't know how alien all this was to her, how aloof she had always held herself from such casual intimacy, how bemused she had felt when friends had tried to explain to her how such sexual intensity felt, how it could overwhelm common sense, caution, and even reality. No, he couldn't know any of these things, and he wasn't going to know. Let him think that, like him, she was simply overwhelmed by the ferocity of the sexual tension which had built up between them.

She felt his hand on her breast and instinctively moved her body to accommodate its touch. A fierce shudder of pleasure ripped through her. She moved closer towards him, shivering as he responded by deepening his kiss, his free hand burrowing under her hair, holding her against his mouth as though he was afraid that she might try to break away.

His mouth tasted of coffee and wine, caressing hers, probing hotly. Her hands curled frantically into his skin as she reacted to the need he was generating.

She had never felt like this before... never... never wanted, ached, needed, *hungered* for a man with this wanton, tormenting urgency.

She felt his hand slide down her neck, searching for the top of her zip, and wanted to tear herself free of her clothes, to feel his hands on her naked flesh, touching her, stroking her, caressing her.

Somewhere in the distance she heard a sound. Muzzily, she opened her eyes. It was the cat, she recognised. She had just jumped in through the window.

Dizzily she focused slowly on him. His pupils were huge and dark, his expression almost ecstatic, drugged...

Her heart missed a beat and then kicked heavily against her ribs. Looking at him, seeing him, watching him, seeing the need she could already feel in his body was so powerfully erotic that she could feel her body responding to it.

'God, I want you.'

She heard him mutter the words and knew they were only an echo of her own need.

She looked at his mouth, watching as it formed the words, and then reached up and touched it with her fingertip, trembling as she felt his lips caress it. Soon now he would pick her up, take her upstairs, undress her and...

She froze as she heard the van driving into the yard. Instantly Richard released her, a dark flush staining his skin as he stepped back from her.

'It's Monsieur Dubois,' she heard herself saying, but she could scarcely recognise her own voice, it sounded so strained and unfamiliar.

Now what on earth had she been doing? How on earth could she have let him... encouraged him...?

A wave of mortification burned through her, her body hot and then cold as the full impact of her own behaviour hit her. It gave her very little comfort to realise that Richard was as stunned and shaken by what had happened between them as she was.

It gave her no sense of triumph to know that physically he was as vulnerable to his desire for her as she had been to hers for him, not even when she could see that, far from revelling in what had happened, he actually looked visibly disturbed, his face drained now that the initial burn of colour had gone.

While he was outside dealing with the farmer, she retreated to her own room. If she had any sense, she would be packing her things now, she admitted to herself, not standing staring into space, but how could she leave when she had given Gale her promise that she would stay? And surely she owed it to her cousin at least to make some attempt to find out if Richard had told George how anxious Gale was to speak to him?

Or was it too late for that? What had happened to her cousin's marriage, that her husband could take time to ring a casual friend and yet could not apparently find time to speak to his wife?

CHAPTER TEN

FROM her bedroom window Livvy could see down into the yard where Richard was talking to Monsieur Dubois. The farmer was talking volubly, gesticulating towards the sky and then shrugging his shoulders before going back to his truck.

Richard watched him go before turning round and walking back towards the house.

As she watched him, Livvy felt the desolation of self-knowledge wash over her.

It wasn't just that she was sexually responsive to him. She loved him. That was why his attitude towards her sex didn't just incite her to defensive anger, but made her ache with pain as well. *That* was why she wanted so desperately to hear him say something, anything which would allow her to believe that beneath his cynicism there were still emotions... feelings, needs.

How *could* she have fallen in love with him? She had always thought of herself as someone who had too much self-regard, too much self-esteem, too much common sense to be drawn into such a potentially destructive situation.

Even if he had returned her feelings. Returned them? Now she was being ridiculous, entering the realms of total fantasy.

He didn't love her. He couldn't love her. He despised her, disliked her... and desired her...

She held her breath as he stood still and looked up towards her bedroom window. Her heart turned over inside her chest.

Yes, there was no doubt at all. She loved him.

She heard him coming upstairs, his footsteps hesitating and then stopping outside her bedroom door. He knocked on it and called her name. Reluctantly, she went to open it.

'That was Monsieur Dubois,' he told her unnecessarily. 'He wanted to warn us about the weather. Apparently bad storms have been forecast and there could be some flooding.'

'But we're too far away from the river here, surely, for it to affect us?' Livvy protested.

'It wasn't the river he was bothered about. It was the lane. It seems that at one time it must have been the bed of a stream. The stream long ago ceased to exist but during heavy storms the lane acts as a natural channel for any flood water and becomes waterlogged. He said something about a tractor...'

'Oh, that must have been the one he wanted Gale to buy. She thought he was trying to palm it off on her and refused.'

She was keeping as much distance between them as she could. She couldn't look at him without remembering how it had felt to be in his arms and how much she had wanted to go on being there... how much she had wanted him.

'We have to talk.'

The quiet words caught her off guard. She looked at him and then flushed, turning quickly away.

'I don't... there isn't...'

'We're adults, not teenagers,' he told her, overruling her stammered denials. 'It's pointless either of us pretending that we don't know what's happening between us.'

Livvy held her breath. Her heart felt as though it had stopped beating, as emotion, shock and hope choked her.

Could she have been wrong after all? *Could* he actually *share* what she was feeling? Could he actually *love* her as she loved him?

She could feel herself starting to tremble, her heart thudding frantically against her ribs as she waited for him to continue.

'Neither of us can deny that there's a certain very strong physical attraction between us—even though it might be something that neither of us wants.'

Livvy felt physically sick. How could she have been so stupid, so self-deluding? Of course he didn't love her, and from what he was saying it was obvious that emotions were the last thing on his mind.

'As I said, we'd be foolish to pretend any different; to ignore what's happening.'

Livvy lifted her chin, her pride smarting from the blow he had just delivered.

'If this is some ploy to persuade me to go to bed with you——' she began, but he wouldn't let her finish.

'Don't be ridiculous,' he told her curtly. 'What I want to do is to make sure that both of us are on our guard to ensure that that is exactly what does *not* happen.

'I'd be lying if I tried to deny the sexual chemistry that's developed between us, but, logically, giving in to it will only lead to complications which neither of us can really want.'

Livvy's face flushed. He was making her feel worse, not better. What kind of man was he, to be able to say openly that he wanted her one minute and then to tell her the next that he wasn't going to do anything about it?

An honest and responsible one, her conscience suggested, but her sense of rejection, coupled with the knowledge of her love, was too strong to allow her to listen to it.

'Your sexual urges might be so strong that you feel you can't exert control over them,' she told him coldly. 'But I assure you that mine are not.'

'No?' he challenged softly. 'Then what was all that about downstairs in the kitchen just now? If Monsieur Dubois hadn't arrived when he did, you know full well I could have had you right there and then, and it wouldn't have mattered a damn if I'd taken you across the kitchen table—to either of us,' he added thickly as the flush which had stung Livvy's face earlier became a searing burn of shocked heat.

Shocked, not just because of what he had said, nor the graphic picture he had drawn for her, but because of her own body's reaction to his words, that sudden, fierce aching pulsing low down in her body which made her want to turn away from him to conceal herself, not just from his eyes but from her own awareness as well.

'As I've just said,' he repeated, 'both of us are too intelligent to pretend it isn't happening, and too adult not to acknowledge the danger.

'Promiscuity and sexual greed are not labels I want to hang round my neck...'

'Meaning that you think *I* do?' Livvy challenged.

Suddenly she was furiously angry, and not just with him but with herself as well. Surely she had the strength of character to recognise how pointless and self-destructive it would be to get any further involved with him?

How much further involved could she be, though? Loving him...

She wasn't going to think about that now. She was going to concentrate instead on denying what he had just said.

'After all, we both know your opinion of me, don't we?' she demanded bitingly. 'I'm surprised that you're prepared to admit to wanting me. Wouldn't it be more in character for you to blame me, to accuse me of trying to seduce you?'

'I wish I could,' he told her flatly. 'At least that way...'

Livvy frowned. Why wasn't he making use of the opportunity she had given him to underline his original condemnation of her? She wanted him to, she acknowledged fiercely, needed him to do so to help her reinforce the wall she was trying to erect between her feelings and what she knew to be reality. The more he showed himself to her as a man it ought to be impossible for her to love, surely the easier it would be for her to get over her ridiculous feelings for him?

'If things continue as they are,' he was telling her, 'inevitably we are going to end up in bed together. It's an explosively dangerous situation, but no matter how good the sex between us might be, we both know...'

Livvy couldn't bear to listen to any more.

'If you're so worried about what might happen, the solution is obvious, isn't it...?'

He looked at her. 'Is it?'

'Yes. *You* must leave. That way there won't be any temptation... any problem... any danger.'

'*I* must leave?'

'Yes,' Livvy persisted stubbornly. 'I was here first and besides, I promised Gale...' She stopped abruptly.

'You're very loyal to her.'

His comment surprised her. 'She needs someone to be,' she told him stiffly. 'It ought to be George... if *he* was loyal to her——'

'Or she to him,' Richard interrupted her quietly.

The way he was looking at her made her heart ache with love and pain. 'I'm not leaving,' she told him shakily. 'You're the one who seems to think... who feels...' She stumbled over the words, unable to find the right ones to express what she wanted to say, and angry with herself for her confusion.

'And you don't agree with me, is that it? Any man, every man could...'

'Why are men always so vain, so obsessed with the power of their sexuality and women's vulnerability to it?' Livvy demanded suddenly, hating him and herself for what he was obviously thinking, for what she by her own actions had *allowed* him to think: that she found him so sexually desirable that she was totally unable to resist him. 'When you first arrived you couldn't wait to tell me that you knew my type, that you considered I was the kind of woman who used sex to barter with, who had so little respect for herself that virtually any man... But now it's different... now suddenly it's *you* who's responsible for arousing my dangerous sexual desires. Do you really, honestly think you're so irresistible? Well, let me tell you, you're not.'

The look he gave her made her eyes burn with shamed tears. He was looking at her as though she had disappointed him, let him down. Didn't he understand that she had had to do it to protect herself . . . to protect them both?

'You know that isn't what I meant at all,' he told her levelly. 'I was wrong in my initial assessment of you, I acknowledge that. It seems I was also wrong to believe that we could talk to one another as two adults, that we both had the maturity to be open and responsible with one another . . .'

He was walking away from her, opening her door and then quietly closing it again behind him.

She'd had to do it, Livvy told herself. She had had no option. So why was she standing here crying, painful, aching tears welling up in her eyes and sliding helplessly down her face? Why had her victory over him left a sour, bitter taste in her mouth?

Was it never going to stop raining? Livvy stared glumly towards the window.

The storm Monsieur Dubois had forecast had broken in the early hours of the morning, the day after her confrontation with Richard. Since then they had each kept their distance from one another, avoiding one another as much as possible. This morning Livvy had hoped to go out, but with the rain so heavy that she couldn't even see across the yard it was pointless even trying to think of doing any sightseeing. She was working upstairs in her room; the kitchen was somewhere she avoided as much as she possibly could do now.

She heard the phone ring and tensed. Richard was downstairs and would answer it. If it was Gale . . . but apparently it wasn't, because there was no foot on the stairs, no voice saying that the call was for her.

She bent her head back over her work and then frowned.

Ten minutes later, when she heard the sound of the BMW's engine being started, she got up and hurried over to the window. Richard was going out. Where on earth to, in weather like this? Was it something to do with the phone call he had just received?

For some reason his absence from the house, instead of helping her to relax, made her feel more uneasy and on edge.

Outside it was murky, no more than half-light, the rain still a heavy, relentless downpour. The cat had taken up almost permanent occupation by the range. It got up and wound itself between Livvy's legs while she made herself a hot drink.

Livvy glanced across at the phone. Perhaps while Richard was out she ought to ring Gale and find out if she had spoken properly to George yet.

She dialled her cousin's number. Roderick answered the phone. He had a cold, he told her, and he was off school. Livvy sympathised and waited for him to fetch Gale.

'Have you managed to speak to George yet?' she asked her cousin when she came to the phone.

'No. It's impossible,' Gale told her fretfully. 'He's still in Japan, out in some remote region where it's impossible to get in touch with him, apparently. The whole situation is ridiculous, Livvy. He's my husband and yet I don't know where he is, or how I can get in touch with him. I haven't seen him for over three weeks. I rang Robert Forrest this morning. Or at least, I tried to. According to his secretary he wasn't there, but she promised she would ask him to ring me.'

'Do you think it's wise tackling him?' Livvy asked her. 'I mean, he *is* George's boss.'

'Exactly. And besides, how else am I supposed to get in touch with George? I've tried speaking to his secretary, but she's useless. Worse than the one he had before and she was pretty hopeless. I told George when he took her on. It was obvious what type she was, although George insisted that her qualifications were excellent. I thought at one time that he might... Well, she was that kind of woman, you know. And they do say that middle-aged men are prone to... But when Robert Forrest took over, she left and this new girl started working for George. I've met her and she's pleasant enough, a world away from the other one, who had vamp written all over her.

'Look, Livvy, I mustn't stay on the phone too long. I'm waiting for Robert Forrest to come back to me... Is he still there, by the way—Richard whatsit?'

'Yes,' Livvy told her. 'Gale, you will let me know just as soon as you have talked to George, won't you? Only it's beginning to be a bit of a strain, staying here, and...'

'Livvy, you *mustn't* leave. You promised me that you wouldn't...'

Livvy sighed.

'You promised me,' Gale reiterated.

'Yes, it's all right. I'll stay,' Livvy assured her.

Five o'clock came and then six. It was almost dark and still there was no sign of Richard's returning.

Make the most of it, Livvy told herself as she made herself something to eat. You're much better off without him here. After all, that's why you want to leave here, isn't it? Because you know how vulnerable you are.

Vulnerable. What had happened to her went way, way beyond that. She could only hope that once she got back to the routine of her normal life she would feel differently. And stop loving him? Was it possible for such a miracle to occur?

She shivered a little and then tensed as she heard a noise outside. It wasn't the noise her ears had been straining for for the last couple of hours, the sound made by a car engine. It hadn't been as definite and audible as that. It had sounded more like someone moving around outside.

She got up and went to the door, opening it hesitantly and then freezing as she saw the apparition walking towards her.

It couldn't be Richard, and yet she recognised that it was, his hair plastered to his skull by the force of the rain, his clothes similarly plastered to his body. There was mud all down one side of him and she could see a tear in his jeans.

'What is it...what's happened?' she asked him anxiously, forgetting their differences as she hurried towards him.

He was limping slightly and, now that she was close to him, she could see a cut on his cheek, still oozing blood, the skin around it already discoloured.

'It's the lane,' he told her tersely. 'It's turned into a quagmire. I swerved to miss a bird—idiotic thing to do— and ended up in the ditch. I tried to move the car but there's no way it can be shifted without a tow. Fortunately it hasn't blocked the lane. I'll give Monsieur Dubois a ring in the morning.'

'So he was right about the tractor,' Livvy murmured. 'You've hurt yourself,' she added. 'Are you all right?'

'Nothing that a hot shower won't cure,' he told her, grimacing as he followed her inside. 'It's just as well your cousin hasn't refurnished this place yet. If she had, there's no way I could go upstairs in this state.'

Livvy could see what he meant. He was already dripping rainwater and mud on to the kitchen floor, and, although he had claimed that he wasn't hurt, the rawness of the gash on his face made her wince sensitively for him.

'Mmm...if Gale were here she'd make you strip off in the kitchen.'

He gave her a brooding look, his voice harsh as he demanded, 'I don't think in the circumstances that that would be a good idea, do you?'

Leaving Livvy staring helplessly after him, he opened the door and went upstairs. She *had* been going to offer to make him a hot drink, but now...

Refusing to let the tears blurring her eyes to fall, she hurriedly cleared away the evidence of her own meal. She was going to go upstairs to her own room, and, when she did, she wasn't going to leave so much as a crumb behind to let him think that she wanted him to be reminded of her.

She was on the landing when the bathroom door opened.

Like a film played in slow motion, she saw Richard standing there, water dripping from his body...his naked body.

'I forgot my towel.'

His voice was blurred and hoarse. It seemed to reach her from a great distance, so that she heard the words but could not shake herself free of the paralysis that gripped her, nor avert her eyes from him.

It wasn't his nakedness that paralysed her, she recognised numbly. It was her own reaction to it; that great tide of shaming, claustrophobic longing and pain which told her with aching clarity just what she was to be deprived of.

Better not to have seen at all than to have to bear the instinctive knowledge that for the rest of her life her flesh would ache weakly for all that it had to be denied, for each touch, each breath, each sensation.

It wasn't a matter of wanting, needing or lusting for him, she recognised fiercely. What she felt went much, much deeper than that.

'Livvy...' She heard him say her name, caught the raw harshness of the word, saw the anger in his expression and turned her back on him, half stumbling in her awkward, anxious attempt to get away.

'Livvy...stop...wait...'

She made a small, anguished sound and then froze with shock as she felt him catch hold of her.

CHAPTER ELEVEN

PANIC overwhelmed her. As Richard turned her round to face him, she lashed out at him, small ineffectual blows which landed harmlessly against his chest. Harmless to him, that was. To her...

As her bunched fingers made contact with his skin, hot and sleek, a silken covering for hard muscles, Livvy started to shake violently.

'Let me go...'

The words threatened to choke her, or was it the tears her pride would not allow her to shed that were blocking her throat?

'Livvy, stop it...listen... Oh, for God's sake.'

She tensed as he picked her up, scooping her off her feet in irritated impatience with her refusal to listen to him, holding her against his body as though...as though he had never spoken those warning words to her, never acknowledged and forced her to acknowledge what was going on between them, but he *had* said those words. Said them and meant them.

It wasn't just she who was tense now. He was, too. She could feel him looking at her and, even though she knew it was the wrong thing to do, the most dangerous thing she could do, she lifted her head and looked back at him.

'Livvy...'

His voice was hoarse, rough, a plea and a demand, his eyes dark with arousal.

When she raised her hands she would have sworn it was so that she could lever herself away from him and put some safe distance between them. So how was it then that, instead of doing so, she was actually allowing them to slide tentatively, caressingly almost, up over his shoulders, her lips parting in a tiny breath, a provocative sigh of wanting as she looked at his mouth?

It wasn't like the other times he had kissed her. This time it was the kiss of a man who already knew he would be her lover, the kiss of a man who desired her and knew that she desired him. It neither forced or cajoled but simply, and far more dangerously, acknowledged and ignited what had already begun between them.

She didn't remember how they had got into his bedroom or on his bed, she didn't remember moving... didn't remember anything at all but the feel of his mouth on hers, the sensation of drowning beneath a kiss so sensual that it stimulated her to a point that was almost unbearable.

She felt him undressing her and even helped him to do it, but it was without any real awareness of what she was doing. All that mattered... all she wanted was for him to continue holding her, touching her, kissing her.

When he broke the contact with her mouth, she whimpered protestingly, nuzzling into his skin, kissing and licking the warm flesh of his throat and then his shoulder, while he groaned in protest and his body arched, his hands holding her briefly away from him.

'I want to feel you against me,' she heard him telling her. 'I want to feel all of you next to me, Livvy... all of you.'

She shuddered mindlessly. That was what she wanted too so why did he... why was he...?

As she felt his hands on her body, she realised he was trying to remove the last of her clothing, the thin cotton all-in-one against which the hard points of her nipples pressed eagerly and wantonly, flaunting their desire for him, so tender that she winced slightly as the soft cotton rasped against them when he removed it.

Instantly his hands were stroking her, soothing her, his lips caressing her swollen, tender flesh, drawing her nipple into his mouth where he bathed it with tender, moist heat.

She started to shiver, wild, fierce spasms of pleasure racking her.

She could hear him talking to her, telling her how much he wanted her, how desirable he found her, how the feel and scent of her body was arousing him, making him want to explore each and every centimetre of her to give her all the pleasure she could ever want.

He wanted her to touch him, he told her; he wanted her to hold and caress him, to feel the need which turned him from a rational human being into something, someone, completely at her mercy and so much in need of her that his senses, his essential being would die of starvation without her to nourish them.

He wanted her, he told her, as he suckled her nipples. He wanted her. His mouth brushed her midriff, her stomach, his tongue circling her navel.

Helplessly, she clung to him, her nails digging into his flesh, stifling the frantic moans of arousal clogging her throat by burying her mouth against him.

He tasted of soap and salt, his skin clean from his shower and yet musky with the scent of his arousal. He groaned when she touched him, smoothing her hand down over his back. His buttocks were flat and hard, the skin slightly paler than the rest of his body where it obviously hadn't been exposed to the sun.

She experienced an unfamiliar erotic urge to trace that demarcation line, to follow it round to the front of his body.

She trembled wildly, molten with pleasure as his hand slid between her legs.

She had wanted him there for so long, touching her like that with sure, knowing fingers that seemed to know all the secrets of her sex and to take pleasure in exploring them.

He reached up to pull her down against him, smoothing the hair back off her face, his own miraculously softened by what they were sharing. She could see desire and need in his eyes, feel it in the response he was making no attempt to conceal from her.

He wanted her to see and know how much he wanted her, she recognised.

Already her body was responding helplessly to his touch, making her arch up eagerly against his hand.

'I warned you it would be like this between us, didn't I?' he groaned as he kissed her. 'I warned you that it would get out of control... That *I* would get out of control,' he added thickly, as she was unable to resist the temptation to reach out and touch him, to caress him as intimately as he was her.

She wanted the taste of him in her mouth, she recognised achingly, the feel of him in her body; she wanted to wrap herself around him and never let him go, to abandon herself completely to him, to be so completely and utterly at one with him that nothing could ever drive them apart.

'Livvy, Livvy...' She felt him shudder as she started to press quick, aching kisses along his body, but when he realised what she was going to do he took hold of her and told her thickly, 'No, no... That pleasure has to be mine.'

And in the end it was his mouth that caressed her with intimate, lingering skill, that caressed and coaxed and finally gave shockingly intense release to her wanton body.

She cried out to him as it happened, clung to him, weeping without knowing why she was doing so.

Later, he made love to her again, filling her with the powerful and longed-for surge of his body within hers.

This time, the release was slower, deeper, and carried with it, for her, an awareness of what this coming together of their bodies was really about, of what lay beyond the immediacy of their physical pleasure, of what this joining of their two physical selves had the power to create.

She wanted him, she recognised, deep within her, was driven to accomplish the satisfaction of that atavistic need not just because of the physical pleasure it gave her.

Nature knew that the closer man's life-force was to its goal, the less distance it had to travel, the higher the chance was of it performing its task, and it was for this reason surely that it had implanted in her the need to urge and incite him to bury himself so deeply within her.

A child...Richard's child; as the waves of pleasure broke inside her, Livvy shivered in feminine awe. That heat she could feel inside her, that ache within her womb...were they just the aftermath of pleasure or were they the beginnings of a new life?

* * *

She fell asleep in Richard's arms, waking up in the darkness some time later, alone and cold.

Shivering, she slid out of the bed. What on earth had she done, and where was Richard? She opened the bedroom door and walked on to the landing, stopping as she heard his voice.

He was on the telephone to someone. She was just about to turn away, not wanting to eavesdrop, when she heard him saying quietly, 'Look, George, it's all right... Everything's going to be all right...'

George... he was speaking to George... George, who could not make time to speak to his wife... George who apparently was too busy and too far away to contact. But not too busy or too far away to ring Richard, apparently.

She was just about to go downstairs and demand indignantly that he let her speak to George when he added, 'I've told you, there's no need to worry about her any more; I'll deal with her. In fact it will be a pleasure,' she heard him saying grimly. 'I know *exactly* what to do to get rid of her.'

Livvy froze; she felt as though the blood had suddenly drained from her body. She started to shake with sick awareness of what she had done.

There was no doubt Richard must be talking about her... that it was her he intended to 'get rid of'. And tonight she had walked right into his trap.

She had to get away from here, she recognised sickly. No matter what she had promised Gale, she couldn't stay now. Not when she knew the humiliation that lay in wait for her. All the time he was touching her, caressing her, *loving* her, in reality he...

Loving her... She shivered violently. Was that really what she had thought? And after all that he had already said to her.

'You fool... You fool...' she taunted herself as she pulled on her clothes and quickly hurried into her own room. She didn't bother trying to pack. She simply grabbed her handbag and headed for the stairs.

The kitchen door was half open. She could see Richard standing with the phone. He had his back to her, thank goodness. So he knew how to get rid of her, did he? Well, she would save him the bother, and the pleasure of further humiliating her. Oh, she could guess how much he would be anticipating that... anticipating reminding her of each whispered self-betrayal, each yearning touch and kiss...each word of longing and need kissed against his skin.

She let herself out of the front entrance of the house. Mercifully it had stopped raining, and the sky was clear, the moon almost full.

Her car was in the outhouse; the engine started first time.

She had just reached the beginning of the lane when the kitchen door was flung open and Richard came racing out.

She could see him in her rear-view mirror. He was calling to her, his shock plainly visible.

So he didn't like being cheated of his plans to humiliate her, did he? Well, tough. She wasn't the kind of woman who would let any man do that to her, no matter how much she loved him.

It must have started raining again, she decided, but when she switched on her windscreen wipers her view was still obscured.

It took her several seconds to realise that she was crying.

She drove slowly down the lane. There was no chance of Richard's catching her after all. She tensed once or twice, wary of skidding on the mud and ending up as he had done in the ditch, but thankfully most of the surface water had drained away and her car was nowhere near as heavy as his.

She had no idea where she was going to go or what she intended to do.

For now it was enough that she had left him. Physically at least.

Emotionally it could take her the rest of her life to forget... Forget... She smiled bitterly to herself... Impossible. She would never forget. Not the pleasure, and certainly not the pain.

She rang Gale from a small village just after dawn, leaving a message on her answering machine saying merely that she was sorry and that she had not been able to stay... That she was all right and intended to use the rest of her holiday to see something of Europe.

After all, what else was there to do? She couldn't go home. Not yet. She needed time and she certainly couldn't go back to the farmhouse.

She drove all morning, stopping only when she recognised that she was virtually falling asleep at the wheel. She had no idea where she was, nor did she really care. She slept in the car and woke up dry-mouthed and feeling dirty.

A few miles further down the road she found an *auberge* where she booked a room.

Luckily the inn wasn't very far from a town, where she was able to buy herself a few basic necessities and a change of clothes. She filled up her car with petrol and made an attempt to eat the meal she had ordered.

What was *he* doing now...? Waiting for her to crawl back to him? Did he know that she loved him? Had he thought that her sexual desire for him would be enough for him to torment her with?

In her imagination, she enacted series of vividly painful scenarios of him laughing at her, telling her he had never really wanted her.

'I'll deal with her,' he had told George, and she had recognised in his voice not just dislike and contempt but an intention to punish as well.

She supposed it was partially her own fault. If she had not been so determined to stand by Gale... And if she had not been so stupid as to fall in love with him.

Hadn't she recognised the first time she saw him that he was a very determined and ruthless man...? *Why* had she been stupid enough to imagine he would allow her to stand between the plans he and George had made?

He wanted the farmhouse, and George wanted to sell it to him. Her presence had made that impossible, and so he had waited and planned and then, when he had finally discovered a weapon he could use against her, he had done so with devastating effect.

'I want you,' he had said, and she had believed him, believed that if there wasn't love then there was passion and need, but his passion had been ignited not by her but by his determination to succeed in removing her.

It was pointless dwelling on all the many small self-betrayals she had made. At least there was one small crumb of comfort. At least she would never have to see him again.

The pain felt as though something was wrenching apart inside her, splintering into a million tiny fragments of individual, agonising pain.

How could she be so weak...so stupid?

She travelled for one week and then another, aimlessly criss-crossing France, instinctively shunning the company of others, snatching a few hours of sleep during the day because she was totally unable to do so at night.

There would not be a child. She told herself she was glad, and for his sake she was, but for her own...

How long was she going to feel like this? Her heart gave her the answer... Forever... Forever.

Three weeks after she had fled from the farmhouse, exhausted physically and spiritually as well as emotionally, she turned the car in the direction of the place that had been her childhood retreat and solace.

None of the family lived there any more, but they were remembered, and Livvy was made welcome, the family who now owned the farmhouse and the land insisting on her staying with them. Their eldest daughter was living in Paris and would not mind her using her room, Livvy was assured. Too drained and weary to argue, she smiled her thanks and allowed herself to be drawn into the warmth of the Gironde family circle.

She could just as easily have walked into the river that ran along the boundary of the farmlands and allowed its waters to close over her head, she recognised dully, but that was a temptation she knew she must resist.

* * *

She stayed in France until not long before the beginning of the new school term.

She had not made contact with anyone at home; she had not felt strong enough to do so. She had worked, though, and she had convinced herself that life must go on, no matter how much of a painful burden she found that knowledge.

She said her goodbyes to the Girondes and headed back for home.

The phone was ringing as she opened the door. She ignored it, grimacing at the amount of mail piled up on the floor and sniffing the stale air of the closed-up rooms distastefully.

Life had to go on. Her pride demanded that it go on.

She froze as one envelope slid free of the others. Her name was written boldly on it. Without knowing how, she knew, she knew that it was from Richard.

She tore it up without opening it. What was the point? All it could do was hurt her even more.

She had things to do... food to buy, bills to pay, work to organise.

The weeks at the farm had tanned her skin, emphasising how slender she had become... How thin... Her hair had grown and needed trimming. Mundane, boring, routine things, the only things that were left in her life for her now.

CHAPTER TWELVE

THE phone was ringing. Livvy tried to ignore it, but the noise persisted. Wearily she pushed aside the duvet and reached groggily for the receiver.

'Livvy, you're back.'

She tensed as she recognised Gale's voice. 'I've been ringing you for days. Where on earth have you been? Why haven't you been in touch? Look, I'm coming round to see you now.'

'Gale, no—I...' Livvy started to protest, but it was too late.

Wearily she got up and padded into her bathroom. When Gale said 'now', now was exactly what she meant.

Livvy was just pouring the coffee into the two mugs she had placed on the table when her cousin's car stopped outside.

Gale looked different, Livvy recognised, as she opened the door to her. Softer, more womanly somehow. Her manner didn't seem to have changed, though.

'Livvy—my God, what on earth have you done to yourself?' she demanded, as Livvy let her in. 'You're far too thin. And where have you been?'

'I'm sorry I had to break my promise to you,' Livvy apologised, as she handed her one of the mugs of coffee. 'But I——'

'Oh, don't worry about that. That's all been sorted out now—Livvy, I've got so much to tell you.

'You remember Robert Forrest, George's boss?'

'The misogynist who took over George's life? How could I forget him?'

'Well, I was completely wrong about him,' Gale told her. 'He's really the most wonderful man... I can't tell you how good he's been. All those things I said about him...I couldn't have been more wrong. He wasn't trying to drive George and me apart at all... he was trying to keep us together. He's totally against divorce.'

'You mean he's totally against other people's,' Livvy suggested drily.

'What?' Gale looked perplexed.

'You told me that *he* was divorced...'

'Oh, yes... Well, I was wrong about that, too. Poor man, it seems that his wife actually tricked him into marrying her by pretending that she was pregnant... It was all a complete fabrication she had hatched up to get at her married lover after they'd quarrelled. It's no wonder it made him bitter.

'Oh, Livvy, I can't tell you what a relief it is to know that George still loves me. It hasn't been easy, I admit. Finding out how close I'd come to losing him, learning that he was... attracted to someone else.'

She bit her lips, her eyes bright with tears. 'Thank God it never got any further than that. Thanks to Robert. If he hadn't acted so quickly... sent George abroad so much...

'I misjudged him totally, you know.'

Livvy stifled her irritation. She was glad for Gale, of course she was, but she was getting a little tired of hearing her cousin sing Robert Forrest's praises.

'You should have got in touch with us, you know. I was worried about you and Robert...'

'I only got back last night, Gale, and I've got stacks of things to do. I'm delighted to hear that you and George have sorted out your differences and that Robert Forrest is such a wonderful, caring human being, but right now...'

Gale's eyebrows rose.

'Well, if that's the way you feel, I suppose I'd better go. What I actually came round for was to tell you that George and I are having a small party on Saturday. It's our wedding anniversary and... You will come, won't you...?'

A party was the last thing she felt like, Livvy acknowledged, but she knew that Gale would nag and persuade her until she gave in and agreed to go.

'All right, but I shan't be able to stay long. By the way,' she added as her cousin finished her coffee and stood up, 'I take it that you and George have sorted out your differences over the farmhouse?'

What was she doing? Livvy asked herself silently. The night she had left him she had sworn that she was putting Richard out of her life, her thoughts, her heart forever, and yet here she was breaking that vow already. It wasn't really the farmhouse she wanted to ask Gale about... It was the man who had shared it with her.

'Oh, yes. It was all a misunderstanding really. George never intended to sell the place. I was furious with him about it at first, but once he'd explained and Robert...'

Robert, Robert, Robert... Here she went again. In George's shoes, she would begin to feel rather worried about the amount of times Gale included his boss in her conversation and her obvious admiration for him, Livvy reflected irritably.

'Of course, Robert will be there at the party,' Gale was telling her now.

'Wonderful. I can hardly wait to meet him. Suppose I'll recognise him by his halo. He will be wearing it, won't he?' Livvy asked her grittily.

Gale was avoiding looking directly at her.

'You've changed,' she accused her, her eyes clouded, and for the first time in her life Livvy recognised uncertainty in her cousin's expression. 'I . . . you know I'd never do anything to hurt you, don't you? That I'd always have your best interests at heart? After all, you are family, and not just that——'

Livvy sighed, recognising all the signs that Gale was about to deliver one of her lectures.

'Tell me about it on Saturday,' she interrupted her firmly, ushering her towards the door and opening it very pointedly for her.

She must have been mad to agree to go to Gale's party, Livvy reflected tiredly as she dried her hair and stared grimly at her reflection. Would other people recognise, as she did, how much she had changed? Would they too see the shadows clouding her eyes, the vulnerability of her mouth, the effect all the sleepless nights and pain of loving Richard had had on her?

They were having an early autumn, the leaves already turning and starting to fall. This morning there had been mist on the fields and the sun, which was shining now, had the pale yellow clarity that said the season had changed.

Livvy discarded the idea of wearing anything summery; it might reveal too clearly how much weight she had lost, and the last thing she wanted was Gale giving her a lecture about it.

Instead, she put on a favourite knitted suit in a soft pale peach. The ribbed top was loose and comfortable, the skirt neat and straight, and although she might be aware that the waistband of the skirt was loose, and that there was more room inside the jumper than there had been, no one else would do so...

Not unless they touched her, that was. But then there was no one in her life close enough to her who was likely to do that, was there? No lover...no partner...no Richard to take hold of her arm and notice its thinness, to place his hand on her waist and recognise how narrow it had become.

Richard... She put down her hairbrush. She was not going to cry...she was not...she must not...she would not, she told herself fiercely.

'Oh, Livvy, good, at last. I was just beginning to wonder where you'd got to,' Gale told her cousin as Livvy handed her the small gift she had bought them and turned to receive George's hug. 'Come on in. You'll know most of the others...'

'Except for Mr Wonderful, of course,' Livvy muttered *sotto voce*, explaining wryly as Gale turned to look at her, 'I was referring to George's boss.'

Gale suddenly looked very flushed and uncomfortable, Livvy recognised.

She frowned. *Was* there more to Gale's admiration of the other man than mere gratitude? Surely not...

'You know, if I were George I think I might feel a little bit resentful of Mr Robert Forrest. He's obviously flavour of the month with you at the moment, Gale.'

'What? Don't be ridiculous,' Gale told her. 'I *am* grateful to Robert, and I do feel guilty about the way I initially misjudged him. You know how I pride myself on being a good judge of character. I feel I owe it to him to...'

'To drag his name into every conversation so that we can all marvel at his metamorphosis from frog to prince?' Livvy questioned her.

'Livvy, I don't know what's got into you. You never used to be like this...' Gale was frowning, looking so worried and concerned that Livvy immediately felt guilty.

'I'm sorry,' she apologised. 'It's just that...' That I'm helplessly in love with a man who doesn't want me... How could she say that? She couldn't, could she?

'It's just what?' Gale pressed her anxiously.

'It's just that I've got a lot on my mind. I still haven't decided what to do about this job.'

'Oh, I see. There's nothing else, then?' Gale asked her.

'What else could there be?' Livvy asked her quietly.

There was an odd look on Gale's face, something almost furtive about her manner.

'Nothing, nothing at all,' Gale assured her hastily. 'There's the doorbell. I'd better go...'

Livvy watched her cousin hurry away with a jaundiced eye.

'Gale, I really ought to go. It's been lovely, but...'

'No. You can't go yet...'

Livvy frowned as her cousin took hold of her arm, almost as though she intended forcibly to prevent her from leaving. 'Gale, I did say I could only stay for an hour or so, and——' She broke off as she heard the doorbell ring.

'Look, just hang on for a few minutes while I go and see who that is,' Gale urged her.

It was easier to give in than to argue. Livvy wandered back into the living-room and sat down in an empty chair.

Livvy could hear the front door opening and Gale speaking to someone, her voice slightly higher pitched than usual, either with excitement or tension, or both.

'Robert... We were just beginning to worry that you might not make it. Was your flight delayed?'

No need to wonder who the new arrival was, Livvy acknowledged grimly. Mr Wonderful himself.

Gale was hurrying into the sitting-room, a tall, dark-haired, dark-suited man at her side.

Richard! Livvy was halfway to her feet without even realising she had moved, her face white with shock and disbelief. Her body felt as though it belonged to a wooden-jointed doll, her movements jerky and unco-ordinated, and as for her heart... her heart was rico-cheting around inside her ribcage, bouncing off the walls of her chest with such high-speed velocity that she ac-tually thought she was going to faint.

Richard... Richard was here!

'Livvy,' she heard Gale saying to her, 'Livvy, I want you to meet George's employer... Robert Forrest.'

Livvy stared at her blankly. No need now to question the guilt and discomfort she could see in her cousin's eyes. No need now to wonder at Gale's odd nervousness and insistence that she didn't leave.

Richard Field... Robert Forrest. *Why* on earth hadn't *she* realised, recognised...?

She felt too sick to move or speak, but Richard—
Robert was moving closer towards her, and if she didn't
do something soon she would be imprisoned...trapped.

She turned to Gale, two angry spots of colour burning
on her cheeks.

'How could you do this to me?' she demanded fiercely.
'How could you...?'

And before Gale could say anything she turned on her
heel, almost running past Gale and Robert, ignoring the
politely curious glances of the other guests and the embarrassed apology George was trying to give her as she
wrenched the front door open and left.

The first thing she did when she got back home was
lock the doors and unplug the telephone, silencing it in
mid ring.

Her stomach was churning nauseously, and she had
the most violently painful headache. Her body seemed
to be out of her own control, and when she turned on
the tap to run some cold water for a drink, her hand
was shaking so much that it took her several attempts
to fill the glass.

Her teeth chattered as she raised it to her lips, and yet
she wasn't cold. In fact she felt almost suffocatingly hot.

Richard was Robert Forrest, and Gale had obviously
known it...known all about his deliberate deceit. And
the rest as well?

No wonder her cousin had been behaving out of
character. Why on earth hadn't she told her...warned
her...?

Because Rich—Robert Forrest had asked her not to.

So much for family loyalty, Livvy reflected sourly, her
top lip curling.

Gale wasn't totally to blame, though. She ought to have guessed that something was wrong. Richard Field...Robert Forrest... She had thought it odd that Gale had not seemed to want to discuss the man whose buying the farmhouse she had been so bitterly opposed to. Knowing Gale as she did, she had half expected her cousin to have something to say about him.

Because of her own anguish, her own fear that Gale might guess what had happened, she had been too grateful to question Gale's unusual silence.

For Gale to *guess* what had happened... Gale already knew, didn't she? Otherwise...

How much *had* he told them? What exactly *had* he said...that he was sorry but he had had to destroy her, Livvy's life? That she had been expendable, an unfortunate victim he had had to sacrifice?

On what? The altar of his own need to revenge himself against her sex? Not because it would in any way aid George and Gale's marriage. She couldn't have made it plainer that *she* wanted them to stay together.

Why couldn't he have told her who he was? Why had it been necessary for him to lie to her about his identity?

Perhaps he had enjoyed deceiving her. There couldn't surely be any other reason.

What difference would it have made to her, knowing that it was Robert Forrest who wanted to buy the farmhouse and not Richard Field?

She frowned... Why, if he had been so keen to preserve Gale and George's marriage, had he deliberately tried to cause problems between them by encouraging George to go behind Gale's back and sell him the property?

She wondered bitterly what Gale would say if she knew the things he had said about her... the criticisms he had made. No doubt she wouldn't think him so wonderful then.

And what had he told them about her? How had he explained her departure?

She had simply left a message on Gale's answerphone saying that she couldn't stay any longer. Had Gale challenged him, asked him why it had been so necessary for her to leave? If she had, Livvy doubted he would have told her the truth.

She tensed as she heard a car draw up outside. The sight of the familiar lean, dark-haired man uncoiling himself from the driver's seat made her shake with nervousness. As she backed away from the window so that he couldn't see her, she saw him pause and look towards her home.

What was he doing here? What did he want? To reassure himself that what had happened between them was something he could safely ignore? To warn her that it had meant nothing and that as far as he was concerned *she* meant nothing?

Her mouth curled into a tight, bitter smile. Did he really think she was stupid enough to *need* that kind of warning?

She heard him knocking on the door but she refused to answer it. It seemed like hours rather than minutes before he eventually gave up and went back to his car.

It was a long time before Livvy got to sleep that night. She lay in bed, her mind churning over and over, and when, just as the birds began to sing the dawn chorus, she fell into a drugged, heavy sleep, it was only to dream

of Richard...Robert...and awaken with red, dry eyes
and a leaden weight pressing down on her chest.

Groggily she crawled out of bed and listlessly made
herself a slice of toast and a strong cup of coffee. Silence
surrounded her, and she sat for what seemed like hours,
staring into space, the toast untouched on her plate in
front of her.

Eventually she remembered that she had unplugged
the phone last night. Her first reaction was to shrink
from replacing the connection—but that was just cow-
ardice, she recognised wearily as she went to reconnect
it. Much as she might want to, she couldn't hide from
the world forever.

It rang, as she had known it would, within ten minutes.

'Livvy?'

'I don't want to talk to you, Gale.'

'Oh, Livvy, look, I *know* how it seems...' Her cousin
sounded really worried, but Livvy wasn't feeling in a
forgiving mood.

'I didn't want to see him again, Gale, and you knew
that. You knew all the time you were telling me about
George's wonderful, wonderful boss what he had done.
You knew as well that if *I* had known who he was there
was no way I'd have been at that party last night.'

'Livvy, please...'

'Don't waste your breath, Gale. I left the farmhouse
to get away from Richard Field...or rather, Robert
Forrest, and no matter what the man calls himself, I still
don't want to see him. *You* might consider that you misjudged him, Gale, but I, on the contrary, believe that
my assessment of him was too generous.'

'Livvy, please try to understand.'

'Oh, I do understand. He apparently went to a good deal of trouble to protect your marriage and you're grateful to him for that. I do understand that. But what I *don't* understand is why protecting your marriage necessitated him lying to me, pretending to be someone he wasn't...'

'He only wanted to help George,' Gale protested. 'To prevent him from falling into the same trap *he'd* been caught in. His wife tricked him into marriage by pretending she was carrying his child. She wasn't pregnant at all, but she had hatched up a plot to force Robert to marry her so she could then divorce him and get a large divorce settlement out of him. She knew the type of man he was and that he would never desert his child.

'He said that the moment he set eyes on Sandra, George's secretary, he recognised that she was the same type as his ex-wife. Apparently she even tried to make a play for him, but he gave her short shrift and sacked her. He tried to warn George, but, as George himself admits now, he was infatuated with her and refused to stop seeing her.

'That was why Robert sent him away so much. He was trying to keep them apart.'

'And why he lied to me about who he was...and threatened you with buying the farmhouse?' Livvy suggested sarcastically.

Gale paused. 'I...I can't explain about that, Livvy. You'll have to ask him those questions yourself.'

'I don't want to know the answers,' Livvy told her curtly. 'I already know as much about him as I want to know...more. He doesn't like our sex, you know, Gale. He's one of those despicable men who have to boost their own egos by putting women down...'

'That's not true,' Gale protested. 'He's been so concerned about you, Livvy. He came straight back to England after you left, you know, and there hasn't been a day since when he hasn't either rung or come round to see if you'd been in touch.

'A man doesn't behave like that unless he cares, Livvy...'

'No? Try substituting "cares" for "a guilty conscience",' Livvy suggested.

'Livvy, I hate to see you like this. Won't you at least see him...let him explain?'

'There isn't anything for him to explain,' Livvy told her fiercely. 'And if he thinks that I'm going to let him manipulate me just so that he can ease his conscience... I don't want to see him, Gale, and that's final. And if that means that I don't see you either, well, then, so be it.'

Livvy could tell from her cousin's silence how much she had shocked her, but she hardened her heart. Gale couldn't know just why she was so determined never to see Richard...Robert Forrest again. It was obvious that she had no idea how Livvy really felt about him. Of course she wanted Livvy to allow Robert to explain and to have everything smoothed over and sorted out, but she couldn't see him, Livvy knew painfully.

She couldn't willingly or voluntarily subject herself to that kind of hurt.

CHAPTER THIRTEEN

ONE more day and then she would be back at work.

Thank goodness. She needed something to occupy her time and her thoughts.

And her heart as well?

Livvy dismissed the thought, stifling the pain that came with it.

She hadn't heard from Gale since Sunday morning and, although she missed her cousin, she was determined not to go back on what she had said.

For so long as Robert Forrest remained a part of her cousin's life, she could not do so.

She stopped her car and got out. The supermarket had been crowded and she felt tired and jaded, her nerves constantly on edge.

Now, as she went to unlock her door, she was glancing over her shoulder as though half expecting Robert Forrest to materialise behind her.

Robert...it suited him. She gave a fiercely bitter shiver. How long was it going to be like this...how long would it be before she finally started to get over him?

Knowing what he was, which ought to have made it all so much easier, might have increased her misery but it had not decreased her love.

She pushed open her door, wincing beneath the weight of her heavy shopping bags.

There was somebody standing in her living-room. A tall, dark-haired man who had no right whatsoever to be there.

As he came towards her, the earth seemed to tilt beneath her feet. She saw the anger in his eyes and made a small helpless sound of pain.

He took the shopping from her, his fingers manacling her wrist as he almost dragged her into her sitting-room.

'Just what the hell are you trying to do with yourself?' he demanded roughly. 'If you lose any more weight, you'll...'

It wasn't her fault she couldn't eat, she wanted to tell him. It wasn't her fault she hurt so much inside, ached so much with the burden of her unwanted love, but stubbornly she held the words back, dragging herself out of his grasp to demand bitterly,

'What are you doing here? How did you get in?'

'Gale gave me her key,' he told her.

Gale... Another betrayal. Livvy stifled her pain.

'She had no right to do that,' she told him stiffly. 'She knew I didn't want to see you. Please leave. Otherwise...'

Otherwise what? Otherwise I might break down completely and tell you just how much I love and need you?

'I'm not leaving until I've said what I've come to say,' Robert told her grimly. 'And you will listen to me, Livvy. You owe me that much at least...'

'Owe you?' She stared at him, fighting down the hysteria exploding inside her.

'Well, don't you? Walking... running out on me like that... What was it you were so afraid of, Livvy? That I might want more from you than you were prepared to give?'

That *she* might want more? He was confusing her, Livvy recognised, deliberately trying to turn the conversation, the situation to his own advantage.

'Why did you lie to me?' she challenged him. 'Why did you pretend to be someone else...?'

'*You* were the one who mistook me for a potential buyer for the farmhouse,' he told her quietly. 'The last thing I'd expected to find when George had given me the keys for the place so that I could have a few days' much needed solitude was to find it already inhabited by a very disturbing and aggressive woman. It seemed more sensible to let you go on seeing me as the enemy...than...'

'Sensible? *Deliberately* to deceive me?'

The look he gave her had something haunted and pain-filled about it.

'Yes, I know,' he said quietly. 'But you see, I didn't know then... You called me a misogynist, Livvy, and it's true that I have felt a certain mistrust of your sex... My marriage...' He shook his head. 'My marriage was something that should never have happened. It was all my own fault. I was twenty-one when Claire and I met; she was slightly older, twenty-four. I suppose I was too young and too idealistic to know what real, genuine love was. Because I wanted her and she seemed to want me, I decided that we were in love. And then she told me that she was pregnant... Carrying my child. We'd barely known one another three months. Foolishly I'd assumed... I think I knew even then, before I married her, that all I'd really felt was physical desire, but she was carrying my child...'

He grimaced painfully. 'Or so I thought... That, like the love she claimed to feel for me, was another fiction, but by the time I realised the truth, by the time she told me that she'd made a mistake and there was to be no baby after all, it was too late and we were married.

'I thought she was as devastated as I was by the way our marriage seemed to be falling apart, but she laughed in my face when I tried to talk to her about it. She told me that the only reason she'd married me in the first place was to get back at her married lover for refusing to leave his wife; that and the fact that I was rich enough to give her a comfortable lifestyle.

'After she told me, I discovered that not only did I not desire her any more, but that it was physically impossible for me to be in the same room with her, never mind actually touch her.

'Then I found out that she had started meeting her married lover again.

'I could have divorced her, of course—I had the grounds—but my pride wouldn't allow me to admit what a fool I'd made of myself, and it didn't suit *her* to divorce *me* ... Not then ... However, all that changed when her lover's wife left him.

'In order to keep everything quiet and discreet, I agreed to the large divorce settlement she demanded... My pride again.

'She died three weeks after the divorce became final ... with her lover ... I felt guilty about that ... the car he was driving had been paid for with the money she got out of me. I felt guilty but I resented her as well for burdening me with that guilt.

'I didn't love her, but I didn't hate her. I did hate myself, though ... I told myself I'd only got what I deserved for being such a fool. That if I'd been less idealistic and more honest with myself, I'd have realised what

I felt for her *was* only desire instead of trying to glorify it...to change it into something it wasn't. I was too proud to admit that I could be that much of a victim to such a basic human drive...that I didn't have more self-control... I swore I'd never fall into the same trap again.

'And then I saw you and there was nothing I could say or do that was strong enough to make me stop wanting you. I was unfair to you, Livvy, totally wrong about you...but please try to understand that was the only way I had of defending myself.'

'Defending yourself? From what?' she demanded.

He looked at her for a long time before saying slowly, 'From loving you.'

'From *loving* me?' Livvy wondered if she was having some kind of hallucinatory fantasy. She blinked and then blinked again, but no, he was still there.

'Stop lying to me, Robert,' she protested huskily. 'You don't love me. You told me in France that you——'

'I told you lots of things,' he interrupted her quietly, 'but those were only words. I thought I'd *shown* you just how shallow and meaningless those words were. I thought I'd *shown* you in my arms just how much you do mean to me...'

'By having sex with me?' Livvy tried to make her voice sound scornful, but it wobbled very betrayingly instead.

'No. By making love with you,' Robert corrected her. '*Why* did you leave like that, Livvy? Have you *any* idea how much what you did has tormented me...how much...?'

'I heard you on the phone to George,' Livvy told him grittily, lifting her chin. 'I heard what you said to him about knowing how to get rid of me.'

Robert was staring at her. She had shocked him now, she recognised, but there was no triumph in the knowledge, only a dull, aching pain that told her how much she had wanted to believe what he had said to her...how much she had ached to believe that he cared about her.

'Yes, that's right,' she repeated. 'You said to George that you knew how to get rid of me...'

'Not *you*... Oh, my God, how *could* you think...? Livvy, Livvy, I was talking about Sandra... That day— my secretary had rung me at the farmhouse; she had strict instructions not to get in touch with me unless it was absolutely urgent.

'Gale had rung her demanding to talk to me about George. I already knew from you how angry she was, and apparently Sandra had been trying to make contact with me as well. I had to speak to George but I couldn't do so with you around, so I drove into town to use the fax machine there.

'When I eventually managed to make contact with George, I discovered that he had come to his senses where Sandra was concerned, but that she was trying to blackmail him over some letters he'd written to her.

'When you heard me speaking to George later, it was *Sandra* I was talking about. Not you.'

Livvy looked at him. She could see that he was telling her the truth.

'But that doesn't alter the fact that you *did* lie to me about who you were,' she told him shakily. 'You say you love me...but how can I believe that when——?'

'I lied to you because I was afraid, Livvy. You see, I knew the moment I set eyes on you how vulnerable I was to you, and the last thing I wanted in my life was that kind of vulnerability. When my first marriage broke up, I swore I'd never allow myself to get involved like that again. I didn't love Claire and it was my pride that was hurt more than my emotions when I discovered the truth about her. My pride that made me determined never to let another woman get close to me.

'I tried to convince myself that you were like her... to deny what I knew was happening to me; and then, when that didn't work, I told myself it was just sex. Even then, though, I knew it wasn't true. If it had been...

'Well, work it out for yourself. If it had just been sex, would I have tried so hard to get you to leave? I knew then, you see. I knew that moment I touched you...held you...

'And then, when it did happen. I didn't even bother trying to fight it...I wanted you too much...'

He had closed the space between them and was reaching out to take her in his arms. Held close against his body, breathing in the wonderful, precious male scent of him, Livvy felt her anger starting to melt away.

'But if I hadn't come upstairs when I did...'

'It wouldn't have made any difference,' he told her. 'Sooner or later it would have happened between us...if not by accident...'

As she lifted her face to look up at him, he smiled at her and bent to whisper something in her ear that made her face flush slightly.

'You see... I would never, never have let you get away from me...and once we had been lovers...

'You do love me, don't you?' he whispered against her mouth, and beneath the words Livvy could hear the hesitancy and uncertainty. It swept away the last of her doubts.

'Yes, I love you,' she whispered back as she clung to him. 'Like you, I didn't want to.'

'But, like me, you've discovered that there are some things, some emotions that we can't control.'

She was still in his arms half an hour later when the telephone started to ring. Reluctantly pushing him away, she told him, 'That will probably be Gale.'

'Tell her you're far too busy to talk to her now,' Robert whispered against her throat. 'Oh, and warn her that she'd better prepare herself for a wedding. A very early wedding...'

Accept 4 FREE Romances and 2 FREE gifts

FROM READER SERVICE

Here's an irresistible invitation from Mills & Boon. Please accept our offer of 4 FREE Romances, a CUDDLY TEDDY and a special MYSTERY GIFT! Then, if you choose, go on to enjoy 6 captivating Romances every month for just £1.90 each, postage and packing FREE. Plus our FREE Newsletter with author news, competitions and much more.

Send the coupon below to: Mills & Boon Reader Service, FREEPOST, PO Box 236, Croydon, Surrey CR9 9EL.

NO STAMP REQUIRED

Yes! Please rush me 4 FREE Romances and 2 FREE gifts! Please also reserve me a Reader Service subscription. If I decide to subscribe I can look forward to receiving 6 brand new Romances for just £11.40 each month, post and packing FREE. If I decide not to subscribe I shall write to you within 10 days - I can keep the free books and gifts whatever I choose. I may cancel or suspend my subscription at any time. I am over 18 years of age.

Ms/Mrs/Miss/Mr _____ EP70R

Address _____

_____

Postcode _____ Signature _____

mps MAILING PREFERENCE SERVICE

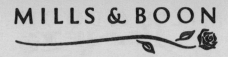

MILLS & BOON

HEARTS OF FIRE by Miranda Lee

Welcome to our compelling family saga set in the glamorous world of opal dealing in Australia. Laden with dark secrets, forbidden desires and scandalous discoveries, **Hearts of Fire** unfolds over a series of 6 books, but each book also features a passionate romance with a happy ending and can be read independently.

Book 1: SEDUCTION & SACRIFICE
Published: April 1994 *FREE* with Book 2

WATCH OUT for special promotions!

Lenore had loved Zachary Marsden secretly for years. Loyal, handsome and protective, Zachary was the perfect husband. Only Zachary would never leave his wife...would he?

Book 2: DESIRE & DECEPTION
Published: April 1994 Price £2.50

Jade had a name for Kyle Armstrong: *Mr Cool*. He was the new marketing manager at Whitmore Opals—the job *she* coveted. However, the more she tried to hate this usurper, the more she found him attractive...

Book 3: PASSION & THE PAST
Published: May 1994 Price £2.50

Melanie was intensely attracted to Royce Grantham—which shocked her! She'd been so sure after the tragic end of her marriage that she would never feel for any man again. How strong was her resolve not to repeat past mistakes?

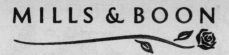

MILLS & BOON

HEARTS OF FIRE by Miranda Lee

Book 4: FANTASIES & THE FUTURE
Published: June 1994   Price £2.50

The man who came to mow the lawns was more stunning than any of Ava's fantasies, though she realised that Vincent Morelli thought she was just another rich, lonely housewife looking for excitement! But, Ava knew that her narrow, boring existence was gone forever...

Book 5: SCANDALS & SECRETS
Published: July 1994   Price £2.50

Celeste Campbell had lived on her hatred of Byron Whitmore for twenty years. Revenge was sweet...until news reached her that Byron was considering remarriage. Suddenly she found she could no longer deny all those long-buried feelings for him...

Book 6: MARRIAGE & MIRACLES
Published: August 1994   Price £2.50

Gemma's relationship with Nathan was in tatters, but her love for him remained intact—she was going to win him back! Gemma knew that Nathan's terrible past had turned his heart to stone, and she was asking for a miracle. But it was possible that one could happen, wasn't it?

Don't miss all six books!

HEARTS OF FIRE

By Miranda Lee

HEARTS OF FIRE by Miranda Lee is a totally compelling six-part saga set in Australia's glamorous but cut-throat world of gem dealing.

Discover the passion, scandal, sin and finally the hope that exists between two fabulously rich families. You'll be hooked from the very first page…

Each of the six novels in this series features a gripping romance. And the first title **SEDUCTION AND SACRIFICE** can be yours absolutely FREE! You can also reserve the remaining five novels in this exciting series from Reader Service, delivered to your door for £2.50 each. And remember postage and packing is FREE!

MILLS & BOON READER SERVICE, FREEPOST, P.O. BOX 236, CROYDON CR9 9EL. TEL: 061-684 2141
